I0549627

Assassins' Canon

Books by Authors in Assassins' Canon

KEN GOLDMAN
You Had Me at Arrgh! Five Uneasy Pieces by Ken Goldman
Donny Doesn't Live Here Anymore
Star-Crossed
Desiree
Of a Feather

DOUGLAS A. VAN BELLE
Barking Death Squirrels

RON SAVAGE
Scar Keeper
Cheap Meat
The Dreaming Field
Loving You the Way I Do: Stories

SUZZANNE MYERS
The Crimson Pact Anthology, Volumes 1-4

S.C. HAYDEN
American Idol
Rusty Nails, Broken Glass

MARK ONSPAUGH
Dark Valentines
Christmas Ghost Stories
Tales from Tomorrow
The Thetis Plague
The Faceless One

CAMILLE ALEXA
Push of the Sky

G. ELMER MUNSON
Tales from the Underground
Stripped

MICHAEL AMOS
Homeland
The Rocktastic Corduroy Peach
The Everlasting Beyond of Eternal Happiness

CHARLOTTE BOND
Hunter's Moon

MURPHY EDWARDS
Dead Lake

KARLA CRUZ
Dog Almighty!

JASON FRANKS
Bloody Waters
The Sixsmiths
McBlack
Lady McBlack
Ungenred

Assassins' Canon

Edited by
EH Rydberg

Utility Fog
Press

First Published 2009 by Utility Fog Press
This edition published 2016

Utility Fog Press
53 Rydal road
Harrogate HG1 4SD
www.utilityfogpress.com

Cover image by Edwin H. Rydberg (http://www.edwinhrydberg.com)

Editorial Staff

E.H. Rydberg	Chief Editor
Alice Shevitz	Assistant Editor
Sarah E. Holroyd	Copy Editor
Stephanie Cassey, Amanda Irazusta, Nicole Smith	Acquisitions Editors

Title font, "Bleeding Cowboys", is used with permission from Guillaume Séguin
(Last Soundtrack, www.lastsoundtrack.com)

Contents

Contents

INTERLUDE

Introduction

Few images evoke a more powerful or frightening reaction than that of the assassin. Silently creeping into your room while you sleep, they plunge a pick deep inside your brain, or fill your snoring nostrils with poisonous vapour. Or perhaps skilled fingers from the shadows strike a vital point during mid-step; the coroners say it was a heart attack. Assassins are people to be feared, no doubt. But what do they fear? What do they dream of? What life, what world, are they longing to achieve with their actions? Is the killing just a job or is there some deeper motivation that drives them? And what happens when it all goes wrong?

Assassins take all shapes and forms with motives and goals as varied as their skills. Some commit gruesome acts with little impact other than for the horror to become burned into our social memory. Jack the Ripper, infamous serial killer of London, terrorized the city for months, killing a handful of victims. His name still lives on in infamy more than a century later, yet the consequences of his actions are felt only in the entertainment industry and the nightmares of children. For others, the deed is clean and focused and earth-shattering in its effect. Gavrilo Princip, largely unknown except to scholars, fired 'the shot heard round the world'. He killed Archduke Ferdinand, initiating World War I, and thereby changing the course of global politics for the next century.

When I began requesting submissions for Assassins' Canon, I had no idea what to expect, but I knew what I wanted. Or, more importantly, what I didn't want. No perfect killers. No James Bonds. No killing with impunity and zero consequence or conscience. Only sociopaths kill with no thought to the consequences. I wanted to explore what is, to me, the more interesting side of the act. What happens when it doesn't go as planned? What about opportunistic murderers, how do they live with themselves afterward? Does the thought always lead to the deed, or can the civilized beast within take the internal discussion further?

Assassins' Canon features opinions from around the world, brought to life in the stories within. In Assassins' Canon a full gamut of would-be killers is explored: gangsters, henchmen, soldiers, newly-weds, the reluctant, the willing, the skilled, and the novice. And, for better or worse, all must bear the consequences of their choices.

E.H. Rydberg
Harrogate, UK 2009

Fat Larry's Night With The Alligators

Ken Goldman

Ken was previously a high school English and Film Studies teacher (Horror and Science Fiction in Film and Literature) at George Washington High School in Philadelphia, Pennsylvania. He is a member of the former GWA, the Genre Writers Association, and an Affiliate Member of HWA, the Horror Writers Association. Ken has published over 485 stories since 1993.

"Fat Larry's Night With The Alligators" first appeared in *Black Moon* #2, September 1995.

Sal turned the Cadillac at Homestead toward Flamingo. He did not say a word to Danny for the next ten minutes. Instead he devoted most of his attention to his meatball sandwich until they passed Long Pine Key. He switched to the dimmers as they approached the park ranger station, but so far they had not seen anything that looked like trouble. From the speakers Tony Bennett crooned something about "Nice work if you can get it" as the Caddy sped past the Pineland Trail turnoff.

Finishing the last of his sandwich, Sal stopped at the Pa-Hay-Okee turnstile of the Everglades entrance station and slid a plastic card into the slot without wiping off his thumbprint of tomato sauce. The crossing bar rose to allow the car through. Danny did not bother to ask his partner how he had managed to get the card. You just didn't question Salvatore DiLucca about something like that.

"Past midnight this part of the turnoff's not meant for anything 'cept marsh rabbits or Seminole Indians," Sal finally said. "Guard your cojones, kid. 'Gators ain't vegetarians." Danny did not laugh. He nodded instead and offered a smile that he hoped did not appear weak.

Once the access road turned to dirt, the body in the Caddy's trunk thumped heavily against the car's frame. It probably would have been easier to haul a Brahma bull into the swamp land. An hour earlier both Danny and DiLucca had had to sit on that lid just to get the damned thing shut. Danny had pumped five bullets into Fat Larry Arnello while the man was still zipping his fly after porking one of Nicky Borelli's whores.

Arnello had made the huge mistake of shaving off a tidy profit from Borelli's Miami cocaine connections while juggling the books he handed to Sal. This had put Salvatore DiLucca in

2

a very bad place with the old kingpin. Every piece man in Miami knew that no one ever got the chance to piss on Sal a second time.

Danny pumped three .45 slugs into Fat Larry's heart and two into his head just as Sal had instructed, but he did not empty the cylinder on him. DiLucca had warned, "You never know when you might need that extra slug." Sal conceded that cutting Arnello's throat may have been more appropriate but why stink up the Cad's trunk? The thought had occurred to Danny to slice off the fat man's pecker and shove it into his mouth just to add a little panache to the job, then figured that might appear a bit hot-blooded for a freshie. It was a clean hit, Danny's first, and whacking that lard-ass proved a lot easier than he had expected. Hell, it even felt good. Nice work if you can get it, just like the man said.

"I'm sure goin' to miss those Arnello dinners," Sal said. "You ever been? No shit, I'd take his wife's lasagna over pussy."

"It's in the meat sauce," Danny agreed absently, still thinking about the swamp alligators and his gonads. He forced himself back into the moment. "Lorraine Arnello does something with the oregano. She wouldn't tell God what's in it if her tits were on fire."

DiLucca nodded before braking so suddenly that Danny pitched forward. Sal pulled the Caddy to the side of the road, cutting the engine and headlights in the middle of Bennett's "No, no, they can't take that away from me…"

The road plunged into darkness. DiLucca looked around and seemed satisfied.

"Sorry about the jolt, kid. It's easy to miss this trail at night." He reached under the seat, handed Danny one of two high-powered flashlights, and pulled the lever to pop the trunk. Danny followed him to the rear of the car while DiLucca looked under the Caddy's trunk lid.

The younger man covered his mouth and gagged.

Fat Larry clearly had seen better days. Arnello's blood had curdled in thick jelly-like pools of fleshy pulp that smeared the plastic shower curtain Sal had used to line the cargo area. But

3

this had not caused Danny's stomach to double over on itself. The stench was another matter entirely.

"Christ, the man is a pig even when he's a corpse," Sal said, assessing the damage done to his trunk by Arnello's posthumous shit. Fat Larry had consumed a truckload of pasta and his sphincter could not hold back the Johnstown Flood his bowels had released. DiLucca covered his nose against the hot stew of spilled guts and turds. "Not exactly a death with dignity, huh, kid? Looks like the plastic caught most of it. Phew! What a stink!"

They spread another plastic curtain on the roadside and heaved the body on top of it, wrapping Arnello inside like a huge cannoli. Carrying Fat Larry past the saw palmetto and strangler figs along the elevated trail was like trying to haul a piano down a sloping mountain. Although it was not far to the river, both men found it difficult to manipulate all that blubber while holding their flashlights steady. The hardwood hammocks served as a marker for Sal who followed the narrowing trail like an Indian scout to the Shark River basin below.

"I know this part of the 'Glades better than most of the 'gators. But be careful, kid. The next log you step on might bite your ass clean off."

The two floated the body about a hundred feet into the marsh through the saw grass where the mangroves grew the thickest, leaving Larry Arnello there like a bloated whale that had swum too close to shore. Climbing back to the elevated boardwalk above the basin they watched the corpse float face down in the hazy moonlight reflecting off the swamp.

"Okay, fellas," Sal whispered to the dark lumps surrounding Shark River. "Soup's on. Tonight you eat Italian!"

They searched the basin and the tall, barbed sedges for motion, their flashlight beams skimming the water-sodden saucer like two lonely beacons.

Nothing moved.

Danny smacked a mosquito off the back of his neck, already sopping with sweat. The sound of swamp crickets rang in his ears, screeching little cooties that did not chirp so much as shriek. The dismal moon crawled behind a dark cloud and

4

winked out, shrouding the river in a blackness so total Danny could feel it inside his bones.

"Christ, Sal. He's floating like a bar of Ivory Soap. You'd think someone so fucking huge would sink faster than a stone."

"He'll go under when he fills up with some of that marsh water. For now it's better he don't. 'Gators feed close to the surface where they can smell what they eat. Ol' Larry is about to become one meat-and-potatoes feast, don't you worry 'bout that."

Turning, Sal's face caught in Danny's flashlight's beam. Danny could see his partner was enjoying this. A smiling Salvatore DiLucca resembled one of those ever-grinning alligators.

Downriver something went *splunk!* Sal aimed his flashlight at the smooth water below the walkway. A dark object that looked like a large tree limb drifted into the beam, barely noticeable in the black ink of the swamp.

From upriver came another splash as a second one, larger than the first, crawled into the water.

The men's flashlight beams circled the basin like searchlights. They sliced through the steamy darkness of Shark River while a galaxy of bugs danced in the glare.

From a small beach about a hundred yards away another alligator charged the water in an awkward motion that looked like a crawl but was much too fast. It belly-flopped into the basin like a clumsy child, vanishing entirely beneath the surface. When it reemerged its awkwardness disappeared as it slid silently toward the body. Only its twin periscope eyes and the upper portion of its back broke the water's surface.

"Come on, guys. That's it, that's it. There's plenty to go around," Sal whispered. "Just a little midnight snack before callin' it a night, hey?"

Danny gasped, aiming the beam at a fourth alligator drifting toward Arnello even closer than the other three. "Jesus! I didn't even hear that one go into the water."

This alligator, larger than the others, probably had entered the river just below the walkway where they stood. Aware of

5

its element of surprise it glided toward its prey faster by keeping mostly underwater.

Four alligators circled the body like a shadowy committee deciding some sort of reptilian pecking order. The large one moved first and fell on Arnello so hard that he disappeared completely beneath the surface. The moment he re-emerged the others went for him. There was no rhythm or pattern to their attack, just the crunch of bone and a constant cycle of tugging and chewing at whatever flesh they could wrench from the body. The attack became a blood-soaked taffy pull as alligators crawled over Arnello and each other, disappearing beneath him, pushing him under the water, then pushing him back up, only to pull him down again. Arnello's arms flailed wildly like a convulsing rag doll and in the wild thrashing it was impossible to tell if the man was a living or a dead thing.

An alligator tugged at his leg, gnawing it into meaty tatters at the knee. It allowed the limb to drift off, favouring another strike at the man's fleshier torso. Another one took a run directly at Arnello's face and managed to remove everything above his nose but an ear that hung ridiculously from a denuded skull. Much of the frenzied attack became lost behind the constant spray of swamp water, and each time Fat Larry re-emerged the twin flashlight beams revealed less of him.

Danny coughed up a taste of his dinner but he chose not to share that information with DiLucca. He snapped off his flashlight and turned away from the scene's bloody denouement.

"In fifteen minutes there won't be enough left of Arnello to spread on a saltine," Sal said, shutting off his flashlight. The sky was swallowed by the thick tangle of slash pines and dwarf cypress, making the darkness complete.

"Are you okay, kid?"

"I'll be okay once we get out of here."

An awkward silence followed. It lingered in the darkness, forcing Danny to focus on the damp reek of the swamp.

"You haven't seen the second act yet," Sal finally added. His voice, emptied of emotion, seemed measured and rehearsed. Danny could barely make out DiLucca's outline silhouetted against the night sky although the man stood close to him. In the darkness he somehow sounded distant.

"Second act?"

Danny snapped his flashlight back on, washing the walkway in light. His partner stood in front of him. He held a gun aimed directly at Danny's heart.

"Sal? What the—?"

"Three words for you, Danny. Just three words." He turned on his own flashlight and held it in front of him to keep a bead on his target.

"Sal, I don't know what you're—"

"You fucked up."

"Sal, what in Christ are you—"

Danny shut himself up. It was pointless to protest further. Still he could think of nothing else to do. DiLucca cut him off before he could utter another word.

"Fucked up big time. 'Til tonight I wasn't sure if Arnello wasn't just tryin' to blow smoke up my ass by fingerin' you as his partner. But when you mentioned Lorraine Arnello's oregano, that sealed it. That ass-wipe wasn't in the habit of invitin' the freshies over to break bread at his wife's table 'less he planned to talk shop over coffee and cigars."

He stepped closer to Danny, the smile melting from his face like a wax candle. Salvatore DiLucca now was all business.

"Fat Larry pocketed Nick Borelli's profits with an accomplice, Danny, someone the traffickers didn't know. I'd hoped Arnello was just tryin' to save his own sorry ass by namin' names. You broke my heart tonight, kid."

A thought formed so quickly in Danny's brain that he acted on it before it had fully taken shape. Talking Sal out of this was not in the equation. He had understood that much the moment he saw the gun.

You never know when you might need that extra slug, kid...

Sal had been so right.

He flashed the high-powered beacon directly into DiLucca's eyes, blinding him long enough to lunge forward and kick the other flashlight off the elevated walkway into the basin below. A bullet tore into his right leg and a searing bolt of pain flashed through the limb. As Danny fell to his knees he tossed his own flashlight over his shoulder towards the swamp, throwing the two men into a darkness devoid of shadows.

Having no better choice in his desperation, Danny rolled off the walkway in an excruciating head-over-heels journey down the embankment to the river's edge. He crawled through a cluster of strangler figs, dragging his shattered leg behind him like a useless pine log.

"I got one bullet left, Sal! Just like you taught me!"

DiLucca fired at the voice coming at him from the darkness below the walkway. The bullet whizzed past Danny's shoulder.

Stupid! Stupid!

Dragging himself into a clump of hammocks in the shallows, he clenched his teeth and waded through the fetid water of the marsh as far as his agony would allow.

Sal fired again and Danny heard the slug plink into the swamp water in front of him.

"I got a whole lot more bullets, kid! A whole lot more!"

DiLucca received no answer. Danny would not be stupid a second time.

"Come on, kid! Take your best shot!"

Still no answer.

A thousand darning needles embedded themselves into Danny's knee. Sal's .45 must have shattered his kneecap and he could not pull himself to his feet without a land mine going off inside his leg. He let the water absorb his weight and he wanted to scream out. Hearing DiLucca step off the walkway, he pushed his way through the hammocks. Maybe Sal was searching for the tossed flashlight. Maybe he was searching for him.

None of this mattered. All Danny needed was one clear shot.

"You're forgetting something, Danny!" DiLucca called out. "You know what it is, don't you? You know what else is out there in that saw grass!"

Danny had not forgotten, but he was a man who had his priorities. Now DiLucca was playing with him, trying to goose him out of the water into the open, trying to get him to say just one word. Sal sloshed through a sea of sedges toward the wounded man concealed by the tall grass in the shallows.

"The alligators, Danny! Hundreds of 'em! They're out there in the dark and you have only one bullet. What you goin' to do, kid? What you goin' to do?"

Danny shoved his knuckles hard into his mouth and bit down on them, trying not to scream. He could not move farther if he wanted to. He would not have moved if he could.

"Remember that quiet 'gator, Danny? The big one you couldn't hear go into the water? Remember what he did to Fat Larry? Maybe that sneaky fucker is crawling through the saw grass toward you right now, lookin' for some dessert! Can you draw that picture in your mind, Danny? Can you hear him comin' for you?"

Danny could. He held the gun out in front of him with both hands, marine-style, wildly searching to his left, then to his right.

Downriver Sal shouted out something that sounded as if he had garbled his words, but Danny could not make it out. DiLucca fired another shot, then two more in rapid succession. If he had emptied his cylinder he would have to reload right there in the swamp water—much too risky a move for a man who did not hold all the cards. This was not Salvatore DiLucca's style.

Unless he was firing at something else!

For several minutes Danny heard thrashing in the water. Then nothing. The stillness surrounding him was worse than anything Sal had screamed out. Danny crouched low in the steamy saw grass waiting for a sound, for something, for anything. His head ached with the riotous chorus of the swamp crickets while a thousand demons did a mad dance inside his brain. In the murky stillness of the Shark River swamp one demon spoke louder than the others.

Why had Sal stopped calling for him?

The saw grass in front of him rustled like crunched paper.

It was crazy to speak, to utter even one word that might give his position away. But the demons would not let him remain silent.

"Sal?"

There was no answer.

9

"Listen, Sal. We can work this thing out!"

Nothing.

The tall grass rustled again. Whatever was there, it was moving closer.

Holding the .45 straight out, Danny aimed it toward the sound of crunching sedges and sloshing water. He waited for the grass curtain to part, knowing that in the next moment either a ravenous 'gator or a man with a gun would emerge. He was ready for either. He could do this.

One shot. Just one shot. If he could keep his eyes on the target right in front of him he could pick it off with one bullet.

"A walk in the park," he whispered to himself. *"Just like a goddamned walk in—"*

The thick saw grass in front of him separated. He held the revolver firm in his grip, one hand steadying the other.

He heard another papery sound, this time from the grass behind him.

Something behind him.

And in front of him.

Danny stared at his hand that held the .45, then slowly dropped his arm to his side. He turned to watch one alligator splash through the grass into the shallows, then two others. They moved in the swamp water in a crawling swim as they circled, watching him, waiting. The grass separated again and two more appeared.

Sal was right. The big one had found him all right, and he had brought his friends.

Danny dug one foot into the soft mud while the other floated uselessly in the murky water. One bullet. One shot. A walk in the park. He could do it.

He could do it.

He placed the barrel of the revolver into his mouth and squeezed the trigger.

No Man's Land

Tyson Young

Tyson Young is an aspiring author living in Ballarat, Australia. He prefers to write thematic, character-driven stories in the realm of speculative fiction, as well as dabbling in a little wacky comedy.

APRIL 22, 1915. THE OUTSKIRTS OF YPRES, FRANCE.

My entire body was submerged in a pit of mud as I lay amongst what had once been green pastures, now beaten to mire by the continuous trudging of soldiers, attacking and retreating, running and dying—a land scarred by death and chaos. Only my face protruded, camouflaged by dry mud and the limbs of surrounding corpses.

From the depths of my muddy cocoon I watched and waited. The mantra of my orders echoed in my mind: eliminate the enemy general—strike the head and the body shall perish.

The thundering of artillery fire, which had been erupting since morning, began to grow sparse, and then ceased altogether as an ominous calm swept over the battlefield. The only apparent noise was the rhythmical pounding of the heart in my chest, thick thuds which reminded me that I was still alive, and that I could die at any moment. Fear gripped me as though it were the cold, dead hands of the fallen men among whom I hid, and the air passed through my lungs with uneven, shuddering gasps.

The clunking of rifles and helmets, the sloshing steps in the muck, and the shaken murmuring and low prayers of German soldiers announced their grim advance from the trenches. I remained motionless, eyes locked in a contest with the sky. Grey clouds passed leisurely overhead, indifferent to the hell that raged below.

Bayonets rose and fell with each uneasy step across the rough terrain. A boot stamped a footprint into the mud next to my face. I listened as a German soldier called to his fellows in a low voice and the men halted around my position. Drawing one long breath, I tried to swallow the fear, and somehow I was able to keep myself from shaking. The soldiers muttered for a moment and then, with a heave, the boot withdrew from the soil, marching towards whatever peril lay ahead.

I had lingered for too long and, securing a hand over my rifle, I rose from the mud like the living dead, clothes smeared in the same bleak grey that tainted every surface of the desolate landscape.

Perhaps there was a reason for this Great War, a noble political objective or some kind of ideal to uphold, but I couldn't see it; I only saw beat-up cannons lying as scrap metal, twisted and broken, unnatural like everything else. Bodies piled all around, blood draining into furrows and ditches, forming rivers of red.

A greater number had perished from pneumonia, starvation, and suicide than from the shelling and gunfire, swamping the area with a foul reek of decay. No vegetation grew in the barren wasteland, for nothing survived there save the flocks of dark birds and vermin and an endless infestation of crawling insects which came in plague proportions to feast upon the fallen. At times I grew to envy the dead. I wondered if there was still a world elsewhere that was worth fighting for—or was it just a memory? Even if I were to return to that world, would it be the same after all I had done and witnessed?

I looked out towards the enemy lines, to a hill a hundred yards away where a man in dull green had been crucified. The body was stretched over a wooden cross, head slumped, eyes closed—long dead. A silent understanding had existed between the opposing forces of No Man's Land, agreeing not to attack during the first hours of light, on religious holidays, or at other inappropriate times. Snipers would not target men who carried out benign tasks such as repairing defences or running messages and water.

Generals were infuriated to discover these unofficial declarations, and so they sought to end any soft-hearted treaties by inciting hatred between the combatants. Perhaps it was under the orders of displeased leaders that the Allied soldier had been so morbidly put on display for all to witness with horror.

I clambered like a dog on its belly, over corpses and under barbed wire, through great craters where men had found their murky graves, mud filling their lungs as they sank under the weight of their rifles and packs. Climbing down a bank, I slid into a shallow brown pool, embracing the security of the cold water. A body floated on the surface, face down, bobbing to the gentle ripples of my movement. With my rifle held overhead, I waded towards the corpse, turning it over and feeling the chill of leathery, purple skin. The man had been a *Feldwebel*—a German corporal, more or less—and by best estimate he hadn't been dead two days. I cut away his pack with my knife and fumbled with the buttons of his overcoat with numb fingers, wrestling his stiff arms from the sleeves. I unfastened his boots and helmet, my bones aching with bitter cold as I replaced my uniform with the dead man's apparel. I never questioned my actions, never thought to be robbing the dead; instead I freed the man of the burdens that made him a soldier, burdens that I would carry in his place, along with the rest of the living who were trapped in war.

I needn't exchange my pants, which were too leaden to recognise, and I kept my rifle, as pilfered weapons were a common sight amongst the ill-equipped trenches. I stumbled up another embankment, peering over to see a channel teeming with smooth grey helmets which rose and bobbed with cautious glances for the enemy—the German front line trench. "Freundlich," I called in immaculate German, waving the confiscated helmet in the air before replacing it on my head. A benign voice called back, and I cautiously poked my head over the ridge before climbing down and into the trench with speed imitating a hasty retreat. My entire consciousness, my every movement, breath, and gesture were regulated to assure those around me of this new identity.

I collapsed against the wall of the trench, feigning exhaustion. Staring at the soil, I wiped the sweat and grime from my brow while attempting to ignore the dozen pairs of German eyes that were upon me. Their gaze did not shift, surveying me as though they could peer into my soul, and so finally I looked up, horrified to see the German soldiers were indeed staring at me—all of them—and that their faces were obscured by strange white masks with goggles, large like the eyes of insects. Rows of cylindrical tanks lay in the trench at their feet, rubber tubes running from the nozzles, up the banks, pointing out toward No Man's Land and the Allied front on the other side. One masked soldier unscrewed the valves of the cylinders one by one, working his way down the line. The nozzles hissed as a white mist escaped, forming a thick vapour that clung low to the ground. So foolishly, I had landed in the trench next to them, completely conspicuous—amidst a gas attack and without a mask.

"Rückseite," one German shouted in a muffled voice. I was paralysed by fear, the kind of hesitation which will get you killed in a second. "Rückseite," he repeated with agitation, motioning for me to move down a rear trench. I suddenly recognised the word, forgotten by fear until then. "Back!" the soldier shouted, warning me from the hazardous gas, for I was not wearing respiratory protection.

"Ja, ja," I nodded, scurrying down the channel, away from the soldiers and toxic canisters. I crawled along a winding canyon towards the support trench, down a flight of rotting wooden planks which sat in the dirt as makeshift steps. A row of German infantry lay prone on an incline, aiming their rifles towards the enemy. Some slumped around a Vickers machine gun, one with his hand poised on the crank. Others wrapped linen gripping around the handles of bats and maces with small iron teeth, or sharpened machetes and sabres. During the day we fought an industrial war, a battle won by automated machines and technology; one machine gun crew could hold off waves of attackers with little effort. At night the combat devolved into primitive, skull-crushing skirmishes under the cover of darkness.

A vast clutter of empty water jugs, ammunition crates, and broken equipment sprawled throughout the trench. Wherever there was space the sleeping or wounded lay, covered by frayed blankets, turning to wheeze and cough. The men were weak, starved, diseased, and demoralised, and yet I found little comfort in knowing that the enemy suffered as we did.

I crouched for a moment, watching the men prepare, trying to make sense of the escalating situation. The Allies were scarcely prepared for full-blown chemical warfare and perhaps my knowledge could have saved many lives. But there was no turning back now, for no doubt my superiors would tell me that this mission trumped the importance of those lives. Duty and honour had lost all meaning in this place; they were mere cues for action. So many lives had slipped through my fingers and I knew that this war, this great thing of destruction and horror, was bigger than me, and far beyond my comprehension. I was a dog, a loyal pet that followed orders and no more than that.

I cursed bitterly, removing my helmet to run a hand through my dirty hair, feeling the weight of my indecision, ultimately aware that I had no control. Perhaps I just wanted to complete the objective and get out of there once and for all, but I couldn't deny that the result of the looming battle was out of my hands.

My allies would have to fare against the gas on their own; the assassination would go ahead as planned.

The trenches were a subterranean maze, and without a panoramic overview it was common for men to lose their way. I wandered deeper, passing an anonymous arm which protruded from one muddy wall. A soldier petted a gaunt German shepherd, clinging to the dog with desperate affection as though it were the very tether of life. He was oblivious to my presence as I passed. I turned into a cramped bunker, in truth no more than a few boards bridging a dead end in the limb of a trench. Crooked sticks and unsteady buttresses reinforced the dirt walls. The uneven shelves held several tins of German rations and corned beef, a delicacy which had been confiscated from the British trenches by German raiding parties. Crates were sparsely filled with medical supplies, broken shovels, rolls of barbed wire, and other equipment—no spare gas masks.

A makeshift desk was covered by old maps that bore little resemblance to the current trench layout after repeated shelling and erosion. I attempted to discern my position nonetheless, tracing my finger from the supply bunker across several zigzagging lines towards the scribbled notation "Viertel des Generals." The General's quarters lay behind a field hospital, well out of range of mortar and sniper fire, and the other vagaries of battle.

I ducked back through the narrow bunker entrance and continued the arduous hike through the lines. Breathing hard, I fought the dull pain that burned in my joints and muscles. Only the knowledge of how close I was to my objective kept me moving. Disquieted soldiers passed by, rifles in hand, flowing towards the front line with apprehensive cries as they prepared for the big push. I came to a rise, and emerged from the trenches where the air was a little clearer, relieved to be rid of the nauseous disorientation of the dirt maze. The crucified man was now only a few yards away, close enough for me to see every gruesome detail and dark vestige of the pain he had suffered.

The explosions and gunfire grew quieter, sounding off on a distant horizon. I had wandered into the ghostly fringes of the battlefield. Passing a row of olive canvas tents, I saw medical staff meander in and out of the marquees, blood up to their elbows. Their strides held no sense of urgency at all, as though they were completely lost. So cold and lifeless, the rear lines almost made me miss the heat of battle.

I pressed on, arriving at a more permanent brick bunker which descended into the earth as deep beneath the surface as some dark cave. Darkness swallowed me whole as I paced down the claustrophobic stairway, each solitary step resounding against the walls. Only a flickering orange glow at the end of the corridor guided me through near pitch blackness. I crept closer, peering into the gloomy chamber.

My target lay right where they said he would be, but nothing else met my expectations. I had imagined a man animatedly barking orders into field telephones and the ears of passing troops, enamoured, and savouring the victory to come as he pushed the Allies back a few yards. Instead the room was devoid of any such spirit or liveliness. A burning torch was held in a sconce in the fashion of a primitive dungeon. The pale figure of a man reposed on a wire frame bed in a corner of the otherwise bare chamber.

From the photos I recalled a soldier who carried himself with all the pride and bravado that accompanied the sharp uniform he wore—all of which had been drained from the pallid face before me. Instead, the General lay decrepit and maimed with disease. Gangrene grew from a shrapnel wound in his leg, which was dressed in soiled bandages. I closed my eyes for a moment, pushing a deflated sigh through my lips, defeated by the knowledge that I had been sent all this way, through peril and hell, to end the suffering of an old, dying man.

I hadn't pictured it to be like this; I hadn't pictured any of it to be this way. I moved forward and reached toward him, yet, as though he detected my movement, his eyelids peeled open. He spoke in German, a low strained whisper.

"Who are you, a dog sent to finish me?" He struggled to utter the words.

I nodded.

"Finally. Finally I can die. I can leave this hell once and for all. I don't want to live in a world where such horrors exist," he muttered, his face distorted by sorrow. "Such...unholy things." The General's glazed eyes were filled with stark horror, a dreadful stare I will never forget.

"Before you kill me, know this...the only crime I ever committed...was that of loving my country," he whispered. I paused for a moment, knowing what needed to be done, yet feeling an inkling of hesitation, that hot sinking feeling. I clasped a hand over his mouth, pinching his nose shut. He tensed up, as if to struggle, but the energy escaped him. My grip remained steadfast, my face stricken of emotion—the whole task was far too easy.

He went limp.

I made the solitary trip up the concrete steps and out of the bunker, emerging in a twilight of yellow haze. The din of shrill cries and desperate screams, the roar of guns and cannons and men all seemed too familiar. I remained for some time, gazing over the battlefield, witnessing the eternal struggle from across a mirror with uncomprehending awe. It was the apocalypse, No Man's Land.

An odd feeling swept over me, as if after all this, nothing had been achieved.

When Love Dies

Jonathan Shipley

Jonathon is a Fort Worth, Texas, writer with fantasy and science fiction stories published in *Weird Tales*, *Dragon Magazine*, *Marion Zimmer Bradley's Fantasy Magazine*, and several anthologies. He is, however, a novel writer at heart and has devoted most of his writing time to a vast story arc that ranges from Nazi occultism, to vampires, to futuristic space opera. "When Loves Dies" was first published in the anthology *Ruins Metropolis* (Hadley Rille Books, 2008).

Danger, instinct told her. Niya's gaze fastened on the port courier hurrying through the holding area on some errand. Their glances crossed momentarily before each of them pulled their eyes away. But it was long enough— the flat, indifferent expression and utterly nondescript appearance told her everything. Guild assassin. She had no doubt that he had recognized her as well.

She was surprised at a guild mission on this backwater world, but the only logic to assassination contracts was money. The door to the hold slid open again and Niya rose from her chair. Two black-uniformed guards from the Church Militant's secular arm dragged Kel into the holding area, dumped him on the floor, and departed.

Drugged, she thought, hurrying over to where he lay sprawled. When he lifted his head, his green eyes swept the area, unfocused and unseeing.

"You shouldn't have resisted," she said, helping him to his feet and walking him over to the banks of plastiform seats. "They wouldn't have resorted to injections if you hadn't resisted."

Kel shook his head. "It doesn't matter. With my metabolism the effects should wear off in—"

"There was no reason for resistance," she interrupted pointedly. He took the hint and fell silent. His brain had to be chemically dulled for him not to realize they were being monitored. The subject of Kel's uniqueness was the last thing they wanted to provide the spy-eyes.

Damn his uniqueness, she thought, studying his unlined face and shock of auburn hair. *In all this time he hasn't aged one day*. Twenty-three years ago she had thought him a precocious youth. Only gradually had she realized he was old enough to be her grandfather. And by then it was too late. She loved him.

Niya liked to think she could have avoided the trap if only she'd known, but she could never be sure. She had saved him from Inquisition imprisonment—by contract, of course. Everything back then had been by contract. She had been a Silence, a guild assassin within the Net of Silence, and she had been primo. Nothing, not even extracting Kel from the security hell of the Inquisition HQ world, had been beyond her. But Kel had been something new in her experience. He had shown her how to grab hold of life and enjoy the ride. But even so she had remained the teacher, imparting her high-level assassin skills to a brilliant student. Then the years had changed even that. He became that rare blend of skill and instinct that every assassin dreamed of becoming. And after two decades, she was past her prime and well past retirement from her erstwhile guild. But still she partnered most dangerously with Kel of the beautiful face and haunting eyes. Even knowing from the start that their relationship was doomed, she might have done nothing differently.

Kel's eyes pulled a little more into focus. "How long can they hold us here?" he asked softly.

"Not more than a few hours," she shrugged. This conversation was for the spy-eyes. "Local law requires that they either charge us or let us go. And of course, we haven't done anything wrong."

He gave her a little smile, just enough to show he enjoyed the irony without being too obvious. They might not have done anything wrong *yet*, but their whole purpose for being on Catmus II was to fan the unrest among the Adorationist underclass. There was supposedly a shrine here—the last vestige of a once-powerful temple complex. It made Catmus a logical point to fan unrest. Once she had been an avid Adorationist, sparing no effort in the quiet war to free her religious brethren, but wild-eyed idealism was beginning to wear thin. Cosmetic rejuvenation to the contrary, she wasn't young anymore.

"Why us, I wonder?" he mused, still playing the game for the spy-eyes.

"They seemed to be strip searching everyone incoming. Maybe the local situation is worse than the vid-reports."

"Well, that's *their* problem, not *ours*," Kel huffed. "I didn't care much for the strip search and I certainly don't think much of their hospitality. Who's in charge here anyway—the local government or the Church? I thought most of the old Adorationist worlds had laws limiting the Secular Arm of the Church. And right in the spaceport—sheez! You'd think they'd at least pretend to follow the rules."

Careful, Kel, Niya thought, keeping her expression neutral. *Don't bait them so openly or we'll never get out of here.*

A few years ago she would have enjoyed the game, enjoyed skirting the edge of danger. All she wanted now was to do the job and go. But go where? They were nomads. They flitted from world to world, nudging and manoeuvring, but they had no real home. The end of one job merely meant the start of another.

She let the conversation die and gave herself over to her inner doubts for a moment. The roller coaster of politics, Church, and nascent revolutions was definitely not enough for her, she realized. Not anymore. Someone had said that middle age hit when a person stopped believing they could change the world. If so, maybe that was where she had arrived. But Kel, like some latter-day Peter Pan, perpetually believed.

The door opened with a *whoosh* and a robed officer stepped inside the holding area. Robed, rather than merely uniformed, implied a rank too high to deal with simple customs offences. "The Inquisitor-Regional is ready to meet with you," he announced, standing aside for them to precede him through the doorway.

Niya saw a quick look of surprise cross Kel's face to be immediately covered with a bland smile. So he had the same question: Why? Nothing in their actions so far should have attracted special attention, but Inquisitors-Regional didn't waste their time on routine interrogations. The most their arrival should have rated was a clerk or guard captain.

24

~

The office of the Church Inquisitor-Regional was appropriately austere with a large plastiform desk and one—and only one—visitor's chair. The Inquisitor himself looked under aged for the position, barely into his thirties. She took that as a sign of ambition.

"Come in, my children," he said, though he was years younger than Niya and who-knew-how-much younger than Kel. They entered, hovering awkwardly over the one chair. All part of the game, she knew, to put interviewees at their worst. She quickly seated herself, beckoning Kel to perch on the arm in a pose much too casual for the game. Then she faced the Inquisitor.

"We have here a problem of sorts," he began with a smile as plastic as his desk. "One that I hope you will be able to clear up for me. It concerns a certain artefact that you were trying to smuggle onto this world."

Kel's mouth quirked into a roguish half-smile, a sure sign he was about to interject some clever impropriety into the interrogation. Niya cleared her throat to head him off. Clever though he was, she was better equipped to argue subtle points of pseudo-law. He cocked an eyebrow at her and stood down.

"Incorrect," said Niya, settling into the calm semi-trance she needed for absolute focus. She gave the Inquisitor a quick smile on the off chance that he might be distractible. She wore her age well, and to the surface observer she still appeared attractive and youngish, if not quite young. A handsome, dark-haired woman in excellent physical shape—that was what people saw. But there was no sign of distraction in their interrogator. "Our luggage invoice specified all items," she continued, losing the smile. "There was no attempt to hide anything."

"But there was deception," insisted the Inquisitor. "All psi-energy artefacts must be specially inspected for clearance. That is the universal rule of the Church."

Psi-energy artefact? She didn't have a clue what he was talking about.

25

"It's just a ceremonial sword," Kel offered with a shrug. "It can't even be classed as a weapon."

He'd slipped a sword into the luggage without telling her? And a loaded one at that, it seemed. Niya's trance wavered in a rising tide of frustration. Why had he deliberately blindsided her? Quickly, she recovered her calm and waded in. Even blind, she could handle this.

"The sword showed no unusual energy readings on any of the standard scans. There has never been a problem with customs on other worlds." Notwithstanding they'd never taken it to other worlds.

The Inquisitor frowned and steepled his fingers under his chin. Kel threw a quick smile of approval at Niya. She pointedly ignored him and waited for the next question.

"Where did you acquire the sword?" asked the Inquisitor after a moment.

"On a primitive world we were visiting," she said without hesitation. "The sword was a gift." It seemed the safest story.

"And you traced its origin?"

"We had no reason to. We suspected that it might be a valuable antique, but as a gift, its value to us was mainly sentimental."

"And the runes on the scabbard and on the hilt? Surely you had them deciphered."

"No," answered Niya, feeling more blind by the minute. Now there were runes as well. "We were not that interested in the runes."

"But you did know they were Runes of Power?"

Oh. No wonder the Church was having a fit. "Of what?" she asked carefully. She would kill Kel later.

The Inquisitor paused a moment, then frowned again. The fact that the Church did not officially recognize Runes of Power—or anything else of Power from the Old Belief—made that line of questioning awkward. "I have no more questions for you at present," he finally said. "But I shall want to talk to you again later."

"Then we are at liberty?" asked Niya.

"Yes. Within the confines of the port city. You shall be apprehended if you try to violate those boundaries."

Kel and Niya left the port complex and headed into the surrounding city. It was low-tech, she realized with a start, despite the presence of a spaceport. But within a few blocks of the port, where Old Town began, there was an abrupt change in technology and architecture. Then, as they continued walking, it changed again—from a sleepy, low-tech sprawl of buildings to a cluster of massive ruins centred on wide boulevards. The old Temple district, abandoned and left to decay, undoubtedly by Church decree. Not a good place for travellers under surveillance to linger.

They backtracked and found a market district with hawkers and street vendors enough to confuse any spy-eye that might still be monitoring them. They wandered, ate meat pastries laden with tart spices, and stopped to watch a street juggler. Just like any tourists.

"Why an Inquisitor-Regional?" Kel asked in her ear, pitching his voice just loud enough for her to hear.

Niya snapped an irritated look in his direction. "Runes of Power, idiot," she murmured back. "That's classified material, even within the Church. It would take someone fairly high up in the Holy Office to handle the interrogation—and it's certainly not over yet." She sighed in frustration. "You could have at least mentioned the sword. I felt like a fool."

"The sword is nothing," he grinned. "But I had to know if I'd gotten the runes correct and a low-level energy scan courtesy of the Church seemed appropriate somehow."

The revelation sank in slowly, triggering first anger that he had gambled both their futures so nonchalantly, then dredging up darker fears. He knew how to set Runes of Power—how was she supposed to deal with that? Was her lover and companion of the past two decades even human?

"You still should have told me," she finished lamely.

"Maybe so," he conceded, "but it's the unexpected that keeps life fresh."

As if instigating rebellion on a powder keg planet wasn't the fast track to the unexpected. He was an idiot— either that or she was too blind to see his latest grand scheme.

27

"But an Inquisitor-Regional?" he added. "There hasn't been any major trouble on Catmus to date. Why is the Inquisition here in force?"

"Just life throwing you the unexpected," she returned with a certain vicious satisfaction. A major Inquisition presence boded decidedly unwell for any political manoeuvring.

Kel grunted and fell silent.

~

Love—betrayal—happy ending. Niya looked up from her holo-drama to find Kel pacing the floor of their rented room. She knew the feeling but didn't have the energy to join him. Since they had checked into the hostelry, the Inquisition had tightened its leash, adding human agents to the surveillance net when their targets chose obscure quarters within Old Town.

Much remained unsaid—that bothered Niya more than the surveillance itself. But all the important questions were too dangerous to discuss at present. Outside the tight information grid of the city, they'd have more options, but for now they were constrained.

She watched Kel continue to pace and knew it wouldn't be long before he launched some daredevil countermove. He hated being restricted, being locked down. Dash in, hit hard, dash out—that was Kel's style. It was the style she had taught him.

Suddenly he stopped. "We have to get the sword back." But the look in his eyes said, 'I'm lying—lie with me.'

Niya switched off the holo-vid. The sword was nothing, he had said so earlier, and it made sense. If he could draw Runes of Power, he could put them on anything. He'd been clever, she had to admit. Using an ancient sword to carry his new runes had neatly deflected the Church's attention in the wrong direction. The Inquisition would be thinking only of the artefact—not its creator—and how it might be used against them.

"If the Inquisition guesses the true power of the sword," she said slowly, "they'll send it offworld. We have to act soon."

Kel's mouth quirked in approval. "Yes, tonight. What about the security codes for the Church compound?"

"I have them. My informant was able to slip me the information when we were in detention." That should cause a stir among their listeners. The Inquisition was notoriously paranoid about its own internal security.

"Removing the sword from its containment field is bound to trigger some sensor, but by then it won't matter. Once I have the sword in hand, all the guards on Catmus won't be able to stop us."

Niya quickly calculated a Church response—a trap with a simulated sword to indict them on charges of security violation without getting into the stickier issues. They would disappear, the sword would disappear, the Church could carry on as usual. Except no one would be walking into their trap.

Kel caught and held her eye. "This is going to be big, Niya," he said, no longer playing only to their audience. "All the Church guards in the sector won't be able to stop what's about to happen."

His words left her chilled, left her dreading the success of the plan as much as failure.

~

Predictably, there was no interference when they left the hostelry after dark and wove a circuitous route through both the port city and Old Town in the general direction of the Church compound. Then on one last weave into Old Town, they quietly slipped into an alleyway, changed into native garb, and melted away into the night in different directions. Within the hour the Inquisition would have a full-scale search mounted, but by then they would be into the outlying districts where spy-eyes would be more conspicuous than effective.

Niya threaded her way through narrow, dirty streets where a lone woman was probably not safe. The thought didn't even slow her step. Any ruffian who marked her as a target would be the one who was not safe. She barely paid attention to the cloaked figures she passed. Then one turned and jumped her.

Dodge, hamstring him, and move on—that was the efficient guild response to unscheduled violence. Any Silence of

29

competence could do so with barely a pause. Niya feinted to the left, at the same time slipping a hand in her jacket to retrieve her quiet ally. A hand from nowhere seized her arm before she found the blade.

A partner? She hadn't noticed that the ruffian had a partner close by, and that was unforgivably sloppy. Now she had to fight in earnest. She yanked her arm away and spun to the side to gain a wall at her back. The partners closed, each brandishing a serrated knife. Her eyes flicked from one to the other—one to keep her occupied while the other came at her from the side. Each with a longer reach and a longer knife than she had. Not good. She felt her pulse and realized she was close to panic. That was even worse. Without focus, she was dead. She took a precious moment to centre herself, then acted.

The palm-blade from her pocket found the throat of the nearer ruffian and he went down gurgling blood. While the other hesitated, she kicked his legs from under him and crushed his windpipe with a quick blow to the throat. While they lay dying on the ground, she dispatched them with their own knives, retrieving hers in the process.

Sloppy, she kept thinking. Forced to kill without a contract. Unthinkably sloppy for a professional…or ex-professional. And her own reactions—sluggish, desperate, panicked. It was their lack of skill, not her own skill, that let her get away from this encounter. Any half-trained assassin-apprentice could have done better.

But let it go. She took a breath to calm herself, then continued on her way. This was only a chance encounter—they had been too clumsy to be Church agents. The business at hand was the Inquisition and local politics. And Kel.

As she made her way through the back streets, Niya's thoughts came back to Kel's words of that afternoon. The pieces of Kel's unspoken plan seemed to be coming together in a way she found unsettling—a large discontented underclass of Old Believers, a stranger appearing in their midst working the old miracles, a sudden cache of rune-empowered weapons. This wasn't just gadflying the Church; this was setting into motion a potential counter-jihad against the Church's incursion into Old Imperial Space.

She reached the abandoned temple district and paused, taking in the shapes of the structures around her to orient herself. The long avenue of massive columns would be the remains of the Processional Way. The original Shrine of the Fire Undying would have been at the far end of the Way, if this temple followed the standard pattern. She hurried in that direction. Midway down the Way, the columns became less jagged and acquired a roof. Some of the carvings were even discernible on the pillars. But this was too obvious, she told herself. If a shrine still existed, it would be anywhere but here. She reached the end of the Way, moved through a wide doorway, and stared down at the oval depression of the Sacred Fire Pit. No fire had burned here in years. Then she became aware of Kel moving along a sidewall. He had reached this rendezvous point some time ago, to judge by his impatient pacing.

"You're slow," he said.

"Yes," she agreed tonelessly, casting her mind back over the street fight. Slow and sloppy. Old. After they slipped past the gateway, she added, "Whatever you have in mind, we need to be careful not to loose a full religious war."

Kel raised an eyebrow. "Or maybe we'll end up right in the heart of one. That's life, I guess."

It wasn't life; it was Kel manipulating everything and everyone—herself included—to produce a particularly bloody result. Looking back at the last few interventions, she could see now that he'd been working up to exactly this all along. But why? He'd never been particularly attracted to violence—given his chosen trade.

Niya levelled a gaze at her companion. "Am I being obscure? Would you like me to repeat that in an Old Iberian dialect? We cannot unleash a full-scale religious war. It's unthinkable."

He gave a boyish giggle, and why not? The professional death-dealer denouncing war. Then he sobered at her expression. "You're serious? We finally get the chance to kick the Church Militant completely off a world and you call it

31

unthinkable? Do you have any idea how long I've waited for this?"

Instead of answering, Niya resolutely looked back along the columned Processional Way. No one had followed—good. Then she sighed. No, she didn't know how long he'd waited. That was a big part of the problem. Kel could have been plotting this for the last century for all she knew. Hell, if he was some sort of immortal witch boy, he could be out to avenge the Old Belief from before the fall of old Tal Imperium. In fact, he could be... Suddenly she didn't want to know; she just wanted out. She wasn't prepared to live her life on that cosmic a scale.

"Well?" prompted Kel. "What's going through that assassin's brain of yours?"

This may have been all he ever really cared about— an encyclopaedic knowledge of dealing death. Niya shook her head. She couldn't let herself believe that. Their relationship might be on the verge of ending badly, but she wanted to salvage the memories.

"There was a guild assassin at the port," she said quietly. "If the guild's involved, we can't afford to—"

"Took care of him," Kel interrupted. "That courier shall carry no more."

When had he done that? When had he had the chance? "That was risky," she pointed out. "Once you draw the attention of–"

"It's happened before," he shrugged. "I don't know if they're after me, but I don't like the coincidence of assassins in my vicinity. Not when I'm working."

There had been others before today...and she hadn't even noticed. But no, they wouldn't be after Kel because he was too difficult, too dangerous a target. They would be after someone less risky, someone whose score needed to be settled. They were there for her. Kel was just prolonging the process.

She watched him stoop and begin tracing something along the edge of the fire pit. Her mouth tightened. He was drawing Runes of Power in a place already sacred and powerful. If he managed to raise the Fire Undying, all hell would break loose. It might well trigger an Adorationist counter-jihad, and the blood would flow. And she didn't want that much blood on her hands.

"You do what you have to on this world," she said abruptly. "I'm pulling out."

Kel looked up from his runes, frowning in disbelief. "What is this, Niya? We've been travelling, working together for years. Why all of a sudden?"

"Because enough is enough without throwing a jihad into the mix." Niya gave a sigh and shook her head. "I'm just tired of it all. Living this way has taken its toll."

His frown deepened. "I don't understand. We make a great team—you, me."

"Kel, look beyond the cosmetic facade. I'm the only person on this team growing old."

He glanced at her as though seeing her for the first time in a long time. "Has it really been that long?" he whispered.

"Twenty-three years, Kel," she answered. "I'm too old to fight this time." *Too old to do anything but drag you down.* "I truly love you. Goodbye."

She said the words, drank in his young, fair face and green-eyed stare for a moment, then turned back toward the city. Better this way so he wouldn't see her continued decline...or find her lying gutted in some back alley by common ruffians.

~

It took a few days to arrange subtle passage offworld through the black market. The Inquisition proved to be less of a problem than she expected but, then again, they had their hands full with sudden eruptions in several rural districts after the Fire Undying had flared briefly but conspicuously in the temple. Niya could see Kel's imprint all over the nightly newsfeeds and found herself secretly hoping for some sign that the operation was going less smoothly than usual, that he needed the old partnership. But she saw nothing to support that hope, just his usual clever manoeuvring. *He never needed me—* the thought kept haunting her.

When she finally shuttled up from the port, she felt more empty than bitter but blamed no one but herself. Only a fool would love an immortal. Unbidden, a line of Church dogma crept into her mind: 'Beware the witchfolk for they will blind your eyes and corrupt your hearts.'

Niya couldn't restrain a little smile. Old and lovelorn she might be, but turning to the Church for wisdom? She didn't feel quite that senile yet.

She looked down on Catmus through the shuttle window for a moment, then abruptly noticed something was not right. The shuttle's weight was insufficient for a smuggling run where every kilo meant extra profit. No smuggler would travel this light with only a lone passenger. Her mind blipped to the abrupt realization that this was a setup, and there was no need to ask more. The courier had had a partner. She had abandoned a guild that tolerated no desertion, and now she would pay the price. It had always been just a matter of time. An undetectable poison in the air supply, she guessed. It would be her choice of deaths for an aging but still dangerous sister-assassin. As deaths went, there were far worse. And she had already said goodbye.

Then she closed her eyes and saw only the green of Kel's eyes and the auburn of his hair.

Fools Rush In, Lunatics Prance

Douglas A. Van Belle

Douglas A. Van Belle is the 2007 Sir Julious Vogel Award (New Zealand) winner for best new talent and was nominated for best novella for 2008. He was also nominated for three awards in 2009. Some of his recent fiction has appeared in *The Andromeda Spaceways Inflight Magazine*, *Sci-Fi Waxes Philosophical*, and *Antipodean SF*.

Few people appreciate how difficult it is to be an evil henchman. In fact, most people try not to think about us at all. Actually, it is worse than that. On the rare occasion that we cross their thoughts, we are nothing but a warm corpse on the pointy end of a sword, a faceless villain to be hunted, or an infestation to be burned out of the rotting detritus befouling a city. Occasionally, someone tries to paint a prettier face over the wrinkles and scars on such a worn out whore of a life, but that's worse than being ignored. Usually it's one of those educated but useless parasites clinging to the fringes of a noble's purse. They spin out tales of secret guilds, honourable thieves, or more fanciful yet, orphans, prostitutes, beggars, thugs, or pirates who use their street skills to rise to respectability or gain some bit of redemption by sacrificing their pitiful lives for the sake of the better people who are worth saving.

For all the good folks, for all those merchants who would never admit cheating a foolish customer, for all those kings who draft conscripts to die in wars over imagined insults, for all those noble wives who occasionally hire one of our ilk to deal with a servant's pretty daughter who might possibly someday catch their husband's eye—those wretched stories teach them to blame us for ourselves. Tales of redemption tell the good people that if we really wanted to, we could choose to join them on the better side. Unfortunately, all that nonsense assumes we had a choice in the first place. No one ever chooses to become a servant to an unsavoury master. No daughter dreams of blossoming into a whore so she can spend every waking hour under one sailor after another. No son hopes to grow big enough for a career breaking the legs of delinquent debtors. Circumstance, fate, and failure conspire to make those choices for you.

For those of us condemned to the underside of life, such ridiculous tales of redemption are worse than a farce. Those stories actually help sustain us in our life of horrible service. They keep that damn dream of an escape alive in our heads. Cruel. Most of us would have chosen death long ago if we could have just extinguished the spark of hope that is perpetuated by those damn stories.

"The planning and logistics for a proper royal wedding take months, Your Highness," I said, trying not to cringe at the effeminate lilt I was adding to my voice. Stereotypes were a dangerous play, so I only used the voice, keeping the words and posture strong, assertive, and masculine. Caricatures came into being for a reason and you had to give the mark something identifiable to latch on to, but it was too easy to arouse suspicion by fitting an expectation too perfectly.

"Thursday," the king commanded, glowering at me with unmistakable and very real annoyance. "Kiri and Connel will marry on Thursday."

"I cannot do anything better in five days than I could in five minutes. You may as well marry them right now. March them down to the docks and stand them in front of a ship's captain. Or better yet, pick a temple and send a soldier down to haul a priest up here so you do not have to interrupt your afternoon's schedule. Hell, you say you are a king. Why put yourself to that much trouble? Just declare them married."

"Why you little…"

The Butchering King of Mandano let the sentence trail off as he rose and pulled his sword from its sheath. The stories about him were undoubtedly exaggerated to the point of fantasy, but like the stereotypes I used, those stories were almost certainly built upon some foundation of fact. I had no doubt that if I pushed him far enough, he would use the weapon. Still, I felt no real fear—you have to care to fear—and without fear it was easy to sustain the bravado. I stuck to the aggressive tack I knew he would choose to respect.

"A royal wedding is a tremendous diplomatic opportunity and if you want to take advantage of that, there must be time. Invitations must go out. Replies must return. Travel must

37

commence. The important guests must be given the opportunity to haul their blubbery arses to the event. Those who need reminding of their place must be given time to hear of the event and become enraged as they wait for an invitation that you choose not to send."

The king lowered the sword, letting the tip drop slowly to rest upon the floor, but he didn't return it to its sheath.

"If you want that, give me the time," I said, staring him in the eye. "If you just want a frilly thing to make your daughter feel pretty, any wench with a flower cart can manage the affair."

There was a long silence before the king said, "When?"

"It will take a week for the invitations to reach all the major kingdoms in the Windward Reaches, a week for guests to arrange affairs and a week for them to travel."

"Three weeks," the king said.

"Summer Solstice," I countered. "It is a little less than four weeks hence. It would add a poetic touch to the event and you could use the wedding to initiate the festival. Tying the wedding to the festival will give you a few more days for diplomatic manoeuvres."

The king gave me a questioning frown.

"Even if a guest could convince the crew of a ship to sail away from the festival, no noble who wishes your favour would dare to insult you by leaving before the celebration had run its full course. A wedding feast lasts an evening at most. The festival will last for two days after the wedding."

"The day of the Solstice." The king nodded and sat back down. "I trust you can reconcile our family tradition of utility and simplicity with a wedding befitting a princess."

"Certainly, Sire."

"You will arrange the affair for half of your requested fee," the king stated, leaving no question that I had no choice in the matter. Turning to his secretary he said, "Send the others away."

I left the king's chamber fending off a touch of despair. I humour myself with jests about playing the character of an evil henchman, but the cruel irony of it all—and there are many cruel ironies involved—is that a truly evil person could never do the job. The sadistic lunatics who might actually desire such an unpleasant task are wholly unsuited to the profession. I have seen those creatures used successfully, but only on the basest levels. Truly evil people enjoy torture too much, so you cannot trust them to use pain to get information directly from a source. However, if you make a show out of feeding a few common criminals to a sadist, the story spreads through the dank confines of a dungeon like the worst of plagues, growing in the fertile imaginations of caged minds denied other stimulation. Sometimes, just the anticipation of such a fate will do the job better than any actual infliction of pain. And if you want to terrorize people and distract a ruler, train a sadist to enjoy the horrific disfigurement of the most innocent of others, then set him loose to prey on the city of a rival. It works. It doesn't accomplish much, but it works and it is about the only thing for which those animals can be used.

For real work, for thinking and acting in pursuit of assigned goals, it takes a real person and for a real person it means a life of despair. A real person must feel despair in the realization of failure and must dread facing the death that failure will inevitably bring. A real person must also still be human enough to feel despair at the thought of succeeding, to find discomfort in inflicting pain and death upon another.

Turning a corner, I collided with a half-naked woman running down the hall. Bouncing off my chest, she giggled as she unsuccessfully fought against clothes that seemed to be trying to crawl off of her extremely robust figure.

She was a beautiful sight but the same could not be said for the insane old wizard who was eagerly chasing her. He looked like a skeleton wrapped in mouldy burlap and just catching a glimpse of him and all his naked glory, prancing and dancing down a brightly lit hall, was enough to turn the stomach of a goat. That vision, in and of itself, might well be regarded as torture.

As the beauty and the old bastard frolicked their way around another corner, my mood spiralled from dim darkness down into a void beyond the deepest black. I was no stranger to dark moods, but that glimpse of the woman, the thought of her with

39

that hairy old bag of bones, put the hammer to an already bleak duty. I crawled back to the inn to wallow in my misery and to wish I could sleep. I couldn't remember the last time I'd had a willing woman.

~

I had succeeded with the first, and perhaps the most difficult, part of my task. There were other options that would have worked if the king had selected another, but this was ideal. Being the royal wedding planner made it ridiculously easy to set up as many options as I thought necessary for completing the task. Still, even after being given quarters in the castle and access to every aspect of the event, the mission was far from complete. I still faced the significant challenge of orchestrating a wedding that was royal enough to avoid suspicion. No small obstacle. I had never even attended a wedding.

I worried myself to the bone about that although, in the end, it wasn't that much of a problem. In the course of faking my way through every profession from potter to priest, I had learned that the best way to look like an expert was to do nothing. All I had to do was find experienced help and let them go. For a royal wedding, I picked the most obvious team of experts.

"I will leave the matter of the dress to your highness and her ladies," I said with a slight bow to the princess. "I am sure that you know best what you would prefer and I expect that you would wish to trust the task to your own dressmaker."

Little girls swirled around the ladies in waiting in a chattering, giggling, squealing pack. Ignorant of any form of protocol beyond the formalities of fighting with siblings, they swarmed around their princess like bees around a hive, interrupting her at their whimsy, hopping up and down in front of her or tugging at her dress when they had to. And when they failed to gain her attention, they resorted to the crazy old wizard. Little better than a child himself, Monty was more than happy to indulge them with his attention or even an occasional sparkle of magic.

Kiri smiled and gave me a slight nod before stooping to address a tiny but persistent child. The child tried to speak but failed, suddenly timid under the princess's gaze. Not the child's fault. Though small herself, the princess was a powerful presence. Every move was graceful and poised; every pose accentuated the other clues to the physical strengths tucked under her skirts. And like her father, she could peer right into you. When they locked onto you those dark eyes of hers penetrated to your very core and demanded the whispers of your soul. And her smile...Her smile was always restrained but it radiated a confidence that unsettled you, and in many ways it was far more effective, far more intimidating and coercive, than her father's threats and scowls. The tiny child's sudden attack of bashfulness could be forgiven. Hell, the only adults who were undaunted by her presence were her father, the old lunatic, and the cocky young wizard she thought she was about to marry.

"We should leave the formal guest lists, seating, and any decisions regarding the assignment of guest quarters to your father's advisors, but I thought we would leave the decorations to the children. On the morning of the wedding we can bring in ribbons, flowers, and other baubles, and let them decorate with the joy and abandon that only a child can offer."

Kiri stood, smiled, and said, "A delightful idea. Perhaps we can do something to ensure that all the children are included."

"Invite all of the local children to decorate the parade route," I put details to her thoughts. "The children of the Mandano nobles can decorate the grand hall for the ceremony, and perhaps the children of the foreign nobles can be given the hall for the wedding feast."

Kiri glanced at Connel before giving me the slight smile that said 'yes'. The young wizard had deferred to her on all of the decisions related to the ceremony, demonstrating wisdom that was unusual for a young man with power.

The couple didn't cling to each other, but it was clear that their betrothal was not an arranged or otherwise mandated affair. They constantly exchanged small touches and their dance of affection was perfectly synchronized. They sensed each other's presence, never stumbling over or clashing with the other.

"The only significant concern that remains for today is the invitations," I said.

"I have already made the invitations," Monty jumped out of a gaggle of little girls, stumbling over one of them and knocking her into a flood of tears and shrill little shrieks of torture. Intercepting Kiri and preventing the princess from attending to the wailing child, the old wizard proudly produced an envelope decorated with swirls that looked like gold but reflected all the colours of the rainbow.

"Monty, that is beautiful," the princess said, not even trying to conceal her surprise that the crazy old wizard had accomplished something a sane person would find appealing.

"Open it." Monty danced and skittered about like a child waiting for the toilet.

Breaking the seal and unfolding the parchment released a flurry of tissue-paper butterflies that fluttered up a few feet before vanishing in tiny bursts of sparkles. The princess smiled; the children squealed. Even Connel nodded, impressed and approving.

"I think we may wish to revise the wording slightly," I said, pointing to the shimmering script. "I think that 'attend or die a miserable death' is stated a bit too strongly and I do not believe we wish to encourage the guests to bring lusty wenches in lieu of gifts."

"We can change that easily enough," Connel said. Wrapping his arms around the princess and pulling her back into his embrace, he set his chin on her shoulder and whispered to her. "Figure out what you want them to say and I will handle it."

"You two do what you wish with them, but they must be ready before the messengers leave on the morning tide."

Unable to ignore their blatant affection for one another, I pretended it was charming and plastered a big fake smile over the darkness that threatened to consume me. Waving at them and the horrible flock of children, I bowed slightly and tried to look a bit harried about the things to be done as I excused myself.

If it were just a matter of killing, my job would have been simple. The princess might be well guarded and Connel may indeed be one of the most powerful young wizards in the Reaches, but I had already passed over at least a dozen opportunities to kill either or both of them and slip safely away. But that was not the point. Killing was not about the dead. Killing was about the effect a death had on those who lived on. Usually that meant that how the target died was as important, or even more important, than actually succeeding. It also meant that there was never anything simple about the planning and execution of the act. The plots to murder nobles were complex because it was about more than gaining access, killing, and escaping. Directing blame, channelling rage, leaving the traces that would hint at but not conclusively demonstrate the motive you wished the survivors to infer, provoking the desired reaction—it all had to be considered in the preparations. If that complexity were not enough, add in the resources and contingencies that must be made available to deal with random events and to allow for whatever improvisation might be needed and, in the end, it would be clear to anyone who cared to actually examine the profession that the comically complex plots of legend and drama were not born of hubris or insanity, but reflected the fact that killing was a means to an end, and that end lay beyond the death of the victim.

Connel, the young wizard of a bridegroom, had given the guest list only the most cursory of glances and had completely failed to notice his hook. I handed the list back to him but chose my words for Michaels, the Captain of the Guard, seated on the other side of the table. "Master Connel, I must insist that you carefully examine and initial each of the guests invited on your behalf. Bribing a clerk for a place on the guest list is the most obvious means of breaching the king's security."

Sighing, Connel took up the list and checked off name after name. With nothing to call a family, his portion of the list was short and once he actually examined it, the omission was obvious.

"Where is Carlis?" he asked. "I know I put Carlis on the list."

"Master Carlis is of a questionable background," Captain Michaels, the King's Captain of the Royal Guard, said gruffly.

The invitations to nobles and other royal guests had gone out days ago. Unlike the personal guests on this list, the risks each of the nobles might present were known and they required only the briefest of reviews. This list required much more careful scrutiny and all it took was a little bit of embellishment to the report on Carlis to push Connel's best friend off of the list.

"Magical ability gives no deference to the whimsy of social status and nobility," Connel said. "Half the wizards in the Reaches are of a questionable background."

"But Master Connel—" Captain Michaels protested.

"Put him on the list." Connel left no doubt it was a command. Technically the young wizard held no rank over the captain, but the soldier knew better than to get too far on the wrong side of the husband of his future queen. When the time was right, Michaels would also remember every detail of Connel's insistence on adding Carlis to the list.

I added the name to the list with my own hand, let Connel finish looking over the list, and then exited with the excuse of needing to rush to get the invitations out. Passing that task off to a clerk, I hurried to the other end of the small castle to put one more foundation stone in place. Quietly slipping into the hall reserved for the rehearsals of the children's choir, I barely bothered to pretend like I was performing my organizational duties as I cut a straight path over to Monty.

"They sing remarkably well for children," I said to Monty as I shouldered aside a few of the young women gathered around the old wizard.

Monty nodded in response, but his attention was on the women. Monty was easy. A simple comment on the quantity and quality of the young nursery maids tending the children had all but guaranteed he would be at the rehearsal.

"With a wizard for a groom, it is too bad that we cannot add a touch of magic to this part of the ceremony," I said to Monty.

That generated some approving coos from the women, and that got the attention of Monty, who looked at me and smiled just a bit.

44

"But the wards protecting the hall will prevent any real magic," I said.

Monty turned to the young blonde closest to him, winked, and with the smallest of movements, shook his head, dismissing the challenge of the wards and protective glyphs in the hall. "The little angels should fly," he said, to her.

Judging from the girl's reaction, Monty's ability and willingness to circumvent the wards were clearly enough to get what he wanted from her, and that would get me what I needed.

The chaos and distractions of the wedding made the rest of the job itself almost simple. With the seemingly endless barrage of tasks that needed my attention, no one noticed the little extra bits I slipped into the mix as I laid out what I needed for not just my primary plan, but also contingency after contingency. With all of the different workers, servants, and even a few early guests trying to stake claims to the handful of unallocated rooms in the castle proper, no one noticed a little man wandering about at night. Further, the guards were quite calm and forgiving on the occasions they caught the harried director of the wedding wandering into places he should not go. Still, as simple as the technical parts were, the charade was so torturous that I found myself constantly doubting success.

"Master Connel. Captain Michaels," I shouted as I ran down the hall. The two men seldom shared each other's company and it had taken far too many days to catch them together.

"Sirs," I said. "I am afraid that Monty fellow has created a bit of a difficulty."

Michaels looked accusingly at Connel, obviously expecting the young wizard to deal with the antics of the old man. From the look on Connel's face, the crazy old wizard had kept him busy.

"Wife or daughter?" Connel asked.

"Oh, no," I said.

Connel raised an eyebrow, quite obviously surprised.

"I mean. I have no doubt he has probably involved himself in plenty of that kind of problem, but that is not my concern." I tried to act flustered at the mention of improprieties. "Master

Monty has decided to add some rather substantial magical enhancements to the performance of the children's choir."

Connel shrugged.

"The protective wards in the grand hall, sir," I prompted him. Wizards could be quite slow at times.

"He will set them off," Connel sighed.

"No, sir, he has removed them."

"The king's hall is exposed?" Michaels, the man personally responsible for the safety of the king and his family, shot a nasty glare at the young wizard. "The wards must be replaced immediately. There must be no magic in the king's hall."

"If I cover the hall with new wards, Monty will just remove them again," Connel sighed. "He may be a lunatic but he is incredibly powerful. Given physical access and a little bit of time, he can and will easily dismantle anything I put in place."

Captain Michaels looked like a nervous dog, caught between conflicting desires and responsibilities. He wanted to run to the Royal Hall and put himself at the king's side, but he knew he was helpless against the magical threats that the wards were meant to protect against.

"I should be able to put something in place that Monty will leave alone," Connel said. "Wards can be focused, so if I surround the Royal Hall with wards directed outward I can build a ring of protection around it. They will stop an attack from outside but still allow Monty to work his little show inside."

Michaels scowled but nodded a reluctant approval.

"The wards you had were marketplace rubbish and needed to be replaced anyway," Connel tried to put a positive spin on the problem. "I can put a far stronger defence in place."

Despite the ease with which I was able to bring all of the parts together, doubts and uncertainties harried me. And the joy of the event was overwhelming. Bursting out from beneath the taciturn edifice of an eternally besieged kingdom, the celebration washed over everything like a lake escaping the grip of an ancient dam. Every smiling face, every flowery symbol of life, every twinkle of hope in a child's eye was a thundering wave, crashing against me. Relentlessly, repeatedly, those waves threw me against the blackness, crushing me against the bedrock that anchored my soul. Even as I felt it beating me down, I could not escape. I could not hide. I was in charge of investing that joy in the event itself and I had no choice but to participate in every detail of the wedding.

If it weren't for the fact that my plan required a whore, which gave me an excuse to risk an evening in the lower quarter, I doubt if I could have managed to sustain the charade. I certainly would have never made it through my last encounter with the princess.

"My lady," I bowed as I entered Kiri's chambers. If she was beautiful before, replacing the simple and functional peasant clothes she preferred with a gown perfectly tailored to her form elevated her well beyond the realm of mere mortals. Even a man who was presumed to have other preferences could be forgiven for a moment of stunned gawking at her beauty.

"Yes," Kiri said, looking slightly uncomfortable as her ladies continued to fuss over details.

I shook away the lustful thoughts and refocused on my task; dwelling on Kiri's beauty would only make it harder.

"I have glued a small coin on the dais to mark the spot where you will wish to stand for the ceremony. You should be able to feel it through your shoe and if you stand on it with your left foot, you will present the perfect profile to the guests."

"Left foot on the coin. Thank you."

She was about to add a comment but a sudden commotion interrupted her.

Completely dismissing any thought of protocol or even manners, Monty and a gaggle of children pushed past the guards and ran into the room.

"Princess," they shouted, almost in unison.

"Yes." She smiled.

"You must have this." Monty held out an ornate and very expensive-looking jewelled pendant. "Something stolen. You are supposed to wear something stolen for the wedding."

"Something borrowed," Kiri corrected him.

"Sure, borrowed," Monty said. "You need to wear something borrowed."

47

"Thank you," she said as she let Monty reach around her to close the clasp on the thin golden chain. "Thank you all," she added for the children.

As the girls danced to the tune of their overflowing excitement, Monty stepped back, assessed the look of the jewellery, and then said, "Perhaps it should be tucked out of sight."

Monty reached out toward Kiri's chest, but she quickly beat him to it, tucking the pendant between her breasts as she scowled at the lecherous old wizard.

Monty pouted like a child caught reaching for a forbidden treat, but withdrew his hand immediately and stepped back.

"And, Monty," Kiri said sternly, almost maternally. "You keep those hands off of my ladies and my bride's maids."

Monty just smiled mischievously.

"Eunuch," Kiri said, threateningly enough to wipe the smile right off the old man's face.

"At your command, my lady." Monty gave her an exaggerated bow and herded the flock of children in angel costumes back toward the door.

The ceremony was beautiful, excruciating. The randomness inserted by the prominent role of the children covered the substantial gaps in my ability, and when Connel's friend Carlis arrived late, still ruffled from the attentions of the whore he thought was the wife of a minor duke, the last piece of my plan was in place. Hovering at the back of the hall, I intercepted Carlis. He was a bit more stubborn than I expected, but after I repeatedly and insistently explained that he was too late and he would disrupt the ceremony if he tried to take his place up front, he reluctantly followed my direction to join the guests relegated to the balcony.

Everything had gone perfectly. All that was left was the timing. I needed to wait until after they were officially married, but that was very near the end of the ceremony and it left only a brief window. The couple had their backs to the crowd during the closing prayer, they faced the throne during the king's blessing, and they would not turn to face the guests until the final song from the children's choir. That was the moment. Everyone would be looking at their faces. The children would scream and shriek. Panic and distraction would help confuse everything, and when the guests trawled back through their memories, they would piece the bits back together in the pattern I had provided.

I gritted my teeth, closed my eyes, and endured, choosing to believe that any who might see me would think I was struggling with the culmination of my responsibilities for the wedding. I had given no one reason to suspect my struggle with the darkness. The vows, the prayer, the king's blessing—I forced myself to return to the wedding as the children rushed past me to take their places for the song. I had my mind refocused on the task as the first of the little angels shimmered in mystical lights and floated up to fly above the princess and her new husband.

Dropping the earring to the floor, I watched the children perform as I waited for the moment.

The earring was the match of the one that my whore had hooked inside the back of Carlis's robe. The witless woman believed the jewellery to be nothing more than an incriminating bauble to be found by a wife caught in some petty game between lusting and jealous rivals, but she could not have been more mistaken. When I crushed its mate under my heel, the earring in Carlis's robe exploded with substantial power.

Carlis yelped and leapt to his feet in reaction to the pain, and at that moment, I said the phrase that triggered the glyphs hidden inside the crude decorations that looked like they had been crafted by the children.

The glyphs sent bursts of cold, unnatural energy lancing down from the balcony. Slashing and ripping rather than burning, they would fling meat and blood out over the guests. That was critical. The princess's blood and pulverized flesh would splatter across the first few rows of guests. The gore should strike every single person of importance to the kingdom. That would make her death more personal than they could imagine. The feel of it striking their skin, the smell, taste, and later, the sight and stench of it when rediscovered on their finest of clothes, would drive the princess's last minutes into their nightmares for months, if not forever, and those last moments would be horrific.

I had purposefully aimed the bursts of unnatural energy to shred the lower half of the person standing on the coin glued to the dais. With her torso left intact she should not bleed to death too quickly and her attendants would rush to her aid. Desperate ladies-in-waiting would try to stop the bleeding, and they might keep her alive long enough for the Royal Surgeon to push his way down from the balcony, but they would be able to do little more than delay her death, and that would only cause more pain to those who watched. Kiri would take several long and agonizing minutes to die. All of the guests would have to suffer through that with her. An eternity to know the reality of impending death, an eternity to stare into the face of that one inevitable fate we all want to deny.

The destruction of such beauty was meaningless by itself. Only in its effect on those who lived did Kiri's death matter. People would scream for vengeance but would be unsatisfied by the worst of reprisals that one man could inflict on another.

With time almost frozen in that instant, I watched the bolts of magic cut through the air. I watched the horror of my own making, but I also felt relief. Until that moment I had managed to keep the image of Kiri's death at bay. If I had allowed that image, if I had admitted that I would be wreaking such ugliness against such beauty, I would have never been able to trigger the glyphs, but I had done it and now I could breathe again.

The sensation of relief, however, was brief. Just as the bolts reached their target they swooped upwards, striking Kiri square in the chest. Her body was flung backward, knocking the priest aside and striking her father a glancing blow before it tumbled down the narrow stair leading to the private offices behind the dais. The slapping of her limbs against the stone caused all to cringe, but it was a swift, clean death—a merciful death.

Though not exactly as I had scripted them, the key aspects of the effect would be close. Every head in the hall swivelled toward the source of the magical attack and every eye locked onto the wizard who had jumped up and yelled. Trial and verdict, the blame fell on Carlis and he would die. That also was only important in the effect it had on others. Connel had insisted on Carlis as a guest. Connel had put the wards in place that allowed magic in the hall, and the young groom would gain so much from the princess's death. He had married himself into the succession for the crown and in the same moment, through the princess's death, he had replaced her as heir. Connel was innocent, but Carlis was Connel's closest friend and his guilt would infect Connel. Connel would bear the blame for her death and the king would be left with no viable choices.

Kiri's death would put an end to any whispers about prophesy, but just as importantly, it would leave a big vulnerable wound in the heart of the Windward Reaches.

Connel put the first of the puzzle pieces together just like everyone else. A searing light burst from beneath the young groom's shirt and he gathered it for a moment in his upraised hands. Then, with a red-faced animal howl, Connel lashed out with magical forces so powerful they distorted the very air in the room. He seized his friend with magical talons, lifted him from the balcony, and shook him like a dog killing its prey. Slamming together two fists of invisible energy, Connel crushed the presumed assassin with nothing but raw magical force. Carlis's bones snapped audibly as his spine and limbs bent in impossible places, the thick, wet noise amplified by the long hesitation as Connel seemed to realize what he was doing. With a stunned look on his face, Connel almost looked surprised as he dropped Carlis's shattered body from near the peak of the vaulted ceiling.

The body hit the stone floor with the slap of cold meat hitting a butcher's block. When Connel saw his friend in the distorted face, the young wizard sagged. He didn't fall, but it was a near thing. Fighting to take a wheezing, strangled breath, Connel turned toward his momentary bride and managed a single step across the dais before collapsing in tears and crawling toward the narrow stair.

The boy had a temper and magical ability far beyond what I had imagined. All the better. People would quickly associate both with a lust for power and the callousness to pursue it. Ironically, the true depth of the young wizard's feelings for

Kiri would make everyone all the more willing to discount his reactions as a charade.

That was when I expected the eruption. Screams, shrieks, and panic should have been breaking free from the shackles of stunned horror. The din should have threatened the foundations beneath the hall and it should have given me more than enough cover for my escape.

Instead, just as the room started to shift toward an eruption, the hint of noise was extinguished by a soft gasp. The whole world was drawn to the back edge of the royal dais where a delicate hand reached up from the stairway that led down to the king's private offices.

Everyone at the front of the hall rushed to Kiri's assistance, but her ladies moved faster than humanly possible, surrounding, protecting, and gently tending to the princess.

Kiri was bleeding from her nose and mouth. The stiffness of her movement hinted at other injuries, but she was clearly alive. She was not only alive, but it didn't look as if she was in any danger of dying. In the brief moment before any of the princess's flock thought to address the lesser concerns of modesty and propriety, I saw the impossible. The magic had not touched her. It had torn the front of her dress away, but even the most delicate bits of the flesh beneath were untouched. She was bruised, so severely bruised that her chest was already turning colour, but the magic of the glyphs I had bought could not have done that.

The last detail to register in my mind was the jewelled pendant, still hanging between her breasts, its gems turned as black as my soul.

My mind raced through the other resources I had hidden for various contingencies. There were knives, darts, poisons, and other items that I might still put to use if I could act before the room settled into the wrong pattern.

I pushed and jostled my way toward the princess as a rough outline of a plan began to take shape, but any hope of salvaging the situation was fleeting. I had options for the failure of the glyphs, for Kiri standing in the wrong place upon the dais, and for just about every possibility other than her surviving the strike.

Monty stepped between me and Kiri, moving with a certainty that left no doubt that he intended to block my way.

"How could someone do this to my wedding?" I squealed, playing out my character as my mind raced through a blur of options that had become little more than wishful thinking.

Monty stared at me. He stared into me and any hint of age or infirmity was washed away by the intensity of those eyes. He had given her that pendant. The flesh-shredding bolts from the glyphs had struck that pendant instead of her legs.

I turned, made a half-hearted attempt to feign distress, and ran from the hall. Down the grand stairway, left into the servant passages, through narrow halls and past heavy doors, I took the shortest and quickest of all the escape routes. Slipping into the crowd of commoners waiting to celebrate the conclusion of the wedding I suddenly, impossibly, found myself once again face to face with Monty. Turning, I lost myself in the buffeting of the crowd, only to catch another glimpse of the old wizard ahead of me. Again and again my path toward the lower quarter was blocked by the impossible appearance of the crazy old wizard. Finally, when Monty stepped out of a doorway to block my way down an empty alley, I gave up, surrendering my fate to his wrath.

"I should have realized you would know the alleys around the brothels," I said as I desperately tried to catch my breath.

"Brothels?" Monty looked around, realized where he was, and laughed. "I have no need of brothels." Pointing up at a small bird flying in a tight circle above the alley he said, "From above, it is quite obvious where you were trying to run."

"Finish this," I snapped.

Monty nodded, gravely, and reached out toward me. I couldn't help but cringe. I had been expecting, in some ways hoping for, my death for as long as I could remember. I knew that this would be merciful, quicker and far less painful than the punishment my master would offer for my failure, but it was impossible not to flinch at the cold, not-quite-burning feeling of the magic penetrating my chest. Monty slowly closed the mystical extension of his fingers around my heart. It didn't hurt. Instead the pressure squeezed the air from my lungs and set my ears pounding. After a moment's hesitation, the old wizard yanked his arm back with all of his strength.

Flesh and bits of ribs exploded from my chest. I dropped to my knees and the pain hit me, like a kick in the chest. Blood poured out of the wound, but my heart still beat. I could still hear it pounding in my ears.

Instead of my heart, Monty held a small black crystal in his hand. It was the leash that tethered me to my unwelcome tasks. It was the talisman that, no matter how far I might run, would burst my heart at the whim of my master.

Monty closed his fist around the crystal and it exploded.

I had seen one of them explode before. I had been forced to watch one obliterate the entire torso of a robust man. At the very least, it should have taken off the old wizard's arm, but it did little beyond making him grunt as he clenched his fist tighter. Smoke from the explosion seeped out of his fist like sand squeezing out from between his fingers, the fire slowly trickling into the air. After a long few seconds, the last of the explosion escaped harmlessly in a shimmer of intense light and the old man relaxed, taking a few deep breaths to steady himself.

"You have two paths," Monty said cryptically.

Struggling to stand, I forced my unwilling legs to support my weight. The wound in my chest was deep and bleeding steadily, but it was small, just large enough for the crystal. I would probably survive.

To my right, the end of the alley framed a view of the castle. I could walk back there and spill my guts. With a little of the king's help I would probably quite literally spill my guts and set at least this one thing right.

I turned and staggered the other way. Redemption would have to wait. For now I would settle for escape. For the few months, weeks, or even days it would take another of my master's henchmen to hunt me down, I would live. For the first time, I would live.

Mullligan and the Serial Killers

J.A. Powell

J.A. Powell is a former Dallas police officer who served as a training officer, detective, sergeant, and commander. Now a businessman in Fort Worth, Jerry restricts his writing to the duration of local timeline shifts, but only after he ensures his grandbabies are safe from the resulting electromagnetic anomalies.

MAY 18, 1985

An hour or so past midnight, Philip Stark, an attorney of some prominence, came upon the Lexus parked at an odd angle. He'd noticed it there when he jogged by the night before, thought he'd heard whimpers, but figured it was the wind. Now, as Phil thought more about it, he became concerned that it might have been someone calling for help. A report to the cops would result in questions regarding his jog at midnight along a Dallas freeway service road since he lived in Carrollton. They might visit the house and his wife would overhear. She would realize he had lied about not seeing Beverly anymore. He couldn't have that. The cost of divorce would be staggering, at least half his fortune. He continued jogging.

MAY 19, 1985

Frank Mulligan placed the fingerprint kit in the trunk as I waited inside the car. While we collected evidence at a 7-Eleven robbery, the busy Saturday night had turned into Sunday morning. As soon as I let the office know by radio we were finished, we caught another crime scene.

"Looks like a homicide at 3400 LBJ Freeway on the north-side service road," said the clerk at CSI headquarters. "Time and date it at 12:30 a.m.; Central Dispatch asks that you contact them for more details."

I acknowledged the call as Mulligan slid into the driver's seat.

"Jack, it's gotta be our killer," he said. "That's right near the sandpile. It's gotta be him."

Almost sixty, he still possessed jet-black hair. It topped a corded face made large by the thinnest frame I had yet seen on a man well over six feet tall.

"You always say that," I said.

"You think it ain't?"

"Nope," I said with a certainty that disturbed Mulligan.

"You may be my sergeant, but you're still a rookie in my book," he said.

I laughed. "Well, we all have to start somewhere."

He laughed, too. "So, you finally acknowledge you're a rookie. It's about time you learned your place, young Jack Goldman. I talked to your dad today, by the way. He says there's hope. Said he finally got across to you what I've been saying to him. You ever wanna make deputy chief like him, you gotta know your place."

Mulligan once ran the Crime Scene Investigations Unit back when it was called the Physical Evidence Unit. He left the department four years ago, not long before I was promoted to patrol sergeant. I got his job by lateral transfer when his successor quit late last year.

My father is Benjamin Goldman, a legendary police officer, now retired. He and Mulligan were lifelong friends. Mulligan watched me grow up, so most of the time to him I was "young Jack Goldman". During a phone call last February, Dad told me he and Mulligan had planned a fishing trip to Colorado. They wanted me to join them. I agreed without hesitation.

As a boy I had tagged along with them when they vacationed in the Arkansas Ozarks. I listened to "Uncle Frank's" CSI tales while we watched our corks bob in the water. Although I majored in physics while in school, I minored in forensics, probably thanks to Mulligan.

On the trip last spring, I learned Mulligan had become bored with retirement. I knew then he still belonged in CSI. He still needed to tell those stories, to figure out how it all occurred, and hopefully, which bad guy did it. So, I talked him into returning as a civilian technician.

He came back cranky, bossy, and always on the lookout for a serial killer. I think he read one too many cop novels while waiting on the fish to take bait.

"Well, geez Jack, did they say if it was under the freeway bridge at the sand-gate or not?" Mulligan asked, now a little irritated.

"They didn't say, but I already know it's not. If I remember right it'll be just down from the exit ramp. The bodies found will be near it, but not in it. So, I don't think it's him."

Mulligan chose not to comment. I suspected he hoped I was wrong so I said, "I worked Auto Theft for two years, remember? The whole city was my beat and I know it like the back of my hand."

Mulligan harrumphed. "Bragging, are you now? Guess I was wrong about you knowing your place."

I laughed again and then he did as well.

We arrived to flashing red lights in every direction. I counted five squad cars and an ambulance surrounding a silver Lexus parked near the outer perimeter of an office complex that bordered the freeway service road. There were dead people inside; we knew that much from Central Communications. Someone had noticed the smell. Some of the night-time office workers who made the original call lingered in the well-lit area adjacent to the Lexus, but the cops on the scene kept them far enough away to avoid problems. The small crowd seemed orderly and obedient.

Mulligan jumped from the car and pulled equipment from the trunk before I could even open my door.

"Sergeant Goldman?" asked an overweight, grey-haired Northwest Patrol division lieutenant as I stepped out.

"That's me." I looked him in the eye only after scanning the scene. There were too many cops.

"I'm Lieutenant Briggs. Mind if I release some of my squads? Dispatch says they got calls waiting all the way to daylight."

I smiled at him. "You can have 'em all back but one two-man car."

"Good deal," said Briggs as he wiped sweat from his forehead with the back of his hand. "I figured Ben Goldman's

58

boy would have plenty of common sense and I was right. I'll leave the first unit on the scene and put the others back in service. You think the same guy done this that killed them others?"

"No, I don't. Five were dumped in water, two buried in those under-bridge sand piles the city uses during ice storms. I doubt it's him."

At that, Briggs seemed relieved. He waved goodbye and signalled to his officers. They were gone in less than a minute. The two uniformed cops who remained stood between the onlookers and the yellow do-not-cross crime scene tape they had originally placed.

Sam Davidson and Mark Sheehan, both veterans of my CSI crew, arrived together in an unmarked, dull-brown sedan and Mulligan barked something at them as soon as they exited the vehicle. They quickened their pace, yanking video and still cameras rapidly from the trunk of their car, then operated with precision.

Mulligan opened the door of the Lexus with a slim-jim while he wore protective rubber gloves. Two bystanders and one of the cops immediately threw up. Mulligan yelled; the remaining cop snapped to and waved away the other bystanders. There was really no need since they were already fleeing the stench of the dead. I'd remembered to soak my nostrils with Vicks.

Mulligan expertly collected samples of hair, blood, and tissue. With each collection, he removed his soiled gloves and placed a clean pair on his hands. Finally, he stood back and surveyed the scene.

"Toss me those tongs and give me a few minutes before you start the vac," Mulligan said to Davidson while staring at the smaller of the two bodies, one that appeared to be a toddler. He used the tongs to pick up a bloody Miss Piggy, placing her in a sack which he lined up in the trunk of Davidson's vehicle with all the other baggies, sacks, and tubes full of collected samples.

The firemen assigned to the ambulance as paramedics looked restless. One of them pinched his nose and asked Mulligan something rather loudly and from a distance.

Mulligan nodded and the ambulance wasted no time departing. Things seemed to get more peaceful when the last of the flashing lights had faded.

The cop who vomited approached, still pale and shaking. I could tell he felt embarrassed, but his uniform remained as impeccable as his haircut. His name plate read John Smith.

He saw me look at it longer than usual and said, "Yep, that's my real name."

I laughed and handed him a wipey from our stock in the glove box. He started to gag again and I held out the jar of Vicks Salve.

"Rub this in your nose. It'll help. Did you run the plate to get the owner's name?"

He nodded, took the Vicks, and did as I suggested as quickly as he could. He caught his breath and said, "Like I told Mulligan, we sent a squad over to the registered address and found the husband. He'd already reported her missing two days ago. Said she and the toddler went to the mall and never came home. He said everything was fine between them, but she was a recovering alcoholic."

"She went on a binge?" I asked.

Officer Smith shook his head and said, "He didn't seem to think so. The last episode happened a year ago, but she never took the baby with her. Looks like she ran into the wrong guy this time. You think he picked her up at the mall? I heard that's where he gets 'em. Maybe he cut her and left her right here? Damn, you think he cut the baby?"

I shook my head. "I'm guessing it's not our guy, but the medical examiner will tell that story. By the way, I don't see his ghouls. Did you call 'em?"

"Sure did, but they only got two wagons working tonight and it's a full moon."

He focused on Sheehan, a bespectacled, intense man who looked more the scientist than a cop. "Why's he setting up the camera on a tripod?"

"He's gonna paint the scene."

"What?" he asked as he cocked a bushy eyebrow.

"He exposes the film over a long period of time. Makes everything crystal clear. We'll paint it from six angles. Takes a lot of time, but that way we can go back to it and spot stuff we might have missed while at the scene."

A look of appreciation appeared on his face. "Well, I'll be. Not bad. I never knew about that."

"It's not something usually known in Patrol unless you draw a lot of homicides. We don't do it at every scene."

Mulligan motioned me over.

"Still think it's him?" I asked.

"Nope, but it might as well be a serial killer."

"Yeah? Why?"

He pointed to various items in Davidson's trunk. "I found a bottle of Jack Daniels on the floor. Her purse, too, and it looked undisturbed. There's plenty of cash in it. It's also got receipts from Neiman's, Brooks Brothers, and Joe's Liquor all dated the sixteenth starting at one o'clock. Then another credit card receipt for lunch and six drinks at Bennigan's restaurant."

"So she did go on a drunk," I said.

Mulligan nodded. "D.L. says she's barely over five feet tall and all of the Jack is gone. Add that to the six drinks at lunch and she couldn't make it home. Must've pulled over on the service road and blacked out. Look how the car wound up being parked. My money's on alcohol poisoning, and she probably died of it right then and there. The child's car seat isn't buckled. Mom was probably too drunk to remember it."

"And the child?" I asked.

"The baby got it worse. I think she suffered all night, then died of heat exposure sometime the next afternoon. Yesterday's temp got over a hundred. That explains the blood, too. Decomposition moved fast and the larger body burst. The alcohol's behind it, though. It's a shame."

"Yeah," I said softly. We wouldn't know for sure until the medical examiner told us, but our job was to make our best guess. Homicide could then decide to wait on the M.E. or move in a solid direction.

"Any decent prints?" I asked.

"One or two so far. Too big of a mess to get much with black powder on this one," he replied.

"Can we generate enough heat inside to use Super Glue?"

When heated in a sealed chamber, Super Glue produces vapours that cling to even the smallest amounts of sweat left behind when fingers and palms touch surfaces. We had rigged several glass chambers back at our lab using light bulbs of various wattages, but a vehicle was a different story.

Mulligan responded, "Yeah, we can put a bowl of it on the middle armrest to centre it up, then hang a heat lamp over it via an extension cord through the windows. We'll seal up the window with duct tape and it'll work like a champ."

Mulligan held out a sealed baggie containing a photograph. The child, dimples prominent on each side of her smile, played amidst bluebonnets in a field as she held an Easter basket while a small woman appeared to clap. She and her mom were dressed identically in pink, and boasted bright blue eyes, visible even from what looked to be an eight-foot camera shot. Both had blond curls that dangled slightly from underneath a red bow of ribbons. He flipped over the baggie to reveal the reverse of the photograph. Handwritten, it read, *Easter Sunday. Joyce and daughter, Becca. "Daddy's Girl"*.

"They're right, you know?" Mulligan remarked as he peeled off his gloves. "Alcoholism is a disease, but I think it's airborne, like the flu, and it infects innocent families like this one."

I looked at Mulligan and then all around as I said, "I've long felt there's more floating on the wind than we suspect. Maybe it *is* airborne."

"Well, if it took the form of a man, he'd be the biggest serial killer of all. One we'd never catch. Shit, most all of us drink, anyhow. I know I need one after looking at this nightmare."

We stared at the vehicle another moment. Mulligan continued, "And another thing. I know it's Saturday night, but look how many cars are blowing by as they exit the ramp. It's a hell of a lot busier during the afternoon, too."

A jogger approached and Mulligan ran to him before he entered the scene. He asked a few short, then longer questions. The body language the jogger displayed indicated he had no wish to cooperate. I got curious and walked over.

The jogger's eyes darted in three different directions every second or so. I motioned Mulligan closer to me and asked him, "He comes by every night?"

"Says no, but he's lying. I can tell. Odd place to be jogging for the first time. His license lists a Carrollton address."

"Name?" I asked Mulligan.

"Philip Stark," he replied and then added, "Esquire." Though most would miss it, I'd known Mulligan long enough to catch the contempt in his voice.

I spoke to the jogger. "Mr. Stark, I'm Sergeant Goldman with Dallas CSI. We're only building facts here, collecting evidence at the scene. We have no problem with you. If you did happen to swing by here last night, it might assist us in determining what happened. Can you help us out?"

The jogger looked down and away and then back at me. He said, "I'm sorry, Sergeant, this is my first time through and the first I've seen of this car."

I read him the same as Mulligan.

I asked Mulligan, "You expected the truth from this guy? Is he married?"

"Says he is."

I stared at the jogger a long moment, and clearly made him uncomfortable. Mulligan seemed to enjoy it. He smirked and turned away to hide a growing smile.

I told Mulligan, "Right now, we've got no reason to hold him. Verify his address with the dispatcher, then give him back his D.L. and send him on. We'll let Homicide stop by his house and have a talk. Make sure you tell whoever gets assigned to check with his wife."

I saw the jogger close his eyes for an instant and slowly shake his head. Although muscular in tone, pretty much in shape, and clad only in a grey muscle shirt and shorts, he still looked soft. Mulligan acknowledged the radio report from the communications officer, waved a dismissive arm, and the jogger took off.

"He says he handles divorces. That's the only part I believed." Mulligan shook his head.

I looked at him. "Just a feeling?"

He ignored me. "I can't believe that guy," he said as he looked at the Lexus, then down the service road. "He might have saved that baby. Even if he didn't see or hear a thing, he could have checked. No telling how many others came by and chose not to check either."

"Maybe there's more than one 'serial killer' in the wind," I said as we watched the jogger disappear into the night.

MAY 20, 1985

The medical examiner's office did a blood alcohol test and reported it to Harold Vance, one of the homicide detectives with whom we closely worked. Harold gave us the preliminary findings. The mother, as we suspected, died of alcohol poisoning.

"He said it's the highest level he's ever measured in a human body that petite at that level of decomposition and he can't figure out how she made it as far as she did. He said the baby died of heat exposure sometime later, probably the next day, but he can't pin it down this early."

Mulligan asked him before I had the chance, "Did you interrogate the jogger?"

"Yeah, we squeezed him some. He needed it. He caved when his wife started raising hell with him while we were there. She ranted and raved about some girl named Beverly until we finally decided to take him downtown and get him to write it all out. He admitted he ran by there both nights prior to the night the bodies were discovered, but he said he didn't see or hear a thing. I asked him why he just didn't stop and check anyway. He said he figured if something was wrong, somebody driving by would have done something about it long before he got there. Said he couldn't be responsible under those circumstances. What a creep. No way we could prove otherwise just by talking to him."

We were silent. We knew what Vance would ask next, "Were y'all able to lift any prints? I'd love to put him touching that car. I'd risk my job to test a negligent homicide case on his sorry ass."

Mulligan looked at me. I nodded and he took the lead.

"We got some," he said as softly as I'd ever heard him speak. I visualized once more the photograph of "Daddy's Girl".

"And?" asked Vance.

"Just a bunch of tiny little hand prints inside, six or seven on every window."

Mulligan said no more. This time he let the evidence tell the story.

Compatibility

Ron Savage

Ron Savage has published more than eighty stories worldwide. Some upcoming and recent publications include *Glimmer Train*, *North American Review*, *Shenandoah*, *The Magazine of Fantasy and Science Fiction*, *Film Comment*, and the *Louisville Review*. Ron has a BA and MA in psychology and a doctorate in counselling from The College of William and Mary.

11:30 AM, SATURDAY
OUR SEVEN ISLAND HONEYMOON CRUISE

Matthew, my new hubby, and I are having cocktails in the Heart of Darkness Lounge, which has your typical Far-Eastern/African motif. The first person I spot is Nicky C—sans wife, of course—with his latest companion. My girlfriend Ro swears this psycho isn't so much mob connected as mob ingratiating. Or, in her words, "Nicky's got Velcro lips." But Ro is a talker, and as much as I love her, you don't talk to a talker regarding the "M" word. Then I see Matt scoping out Nicky C's companion. The woman has had at least sixty, seventy-five thousand dollars worth of cosmetic work done. She looks like a Barbie minus the personality.

I say, "You like that type, hon?"

"Are they real?"

Matthew and I met online, at one of those dot-com places, where they give you a personality test then match your score up with the individual best suited to your true inner self. I didn't even have to leave my condo. Believe me, it's amazing. Two months later, we're married, no muss, no fuss. Basically, my mother said, "Oh, *God*, Gennine, I hope you know what you're doing."

Right now I'm giving Matt The Look. He says that by "real", he means the jewellery. That's definitely Nicky C's redeeming quality. He keeps a running tab at Tiffany's and a couple of stores in the diamond district. The man may kill and maim, but he knows his precious gems. The piece currently hanging around Ms. Barbie's neck is a collar of sapphires the size of babies' thumbs surrounded by diamonds—*with* matching earrings.

"I like his style," my hubby says.

Matthew hasn't asked me what I do for a living, and I certainly haven't pried into his life, either. When we decided to take the cruise, he paid the travel agent in cash. Matt has that sexy accountant thing, if you'll excuse the oxymoron. He's slim, balding slightly, wears lots of nice suits, Ralph Lauren, Joseph Abboud, *et cetera*, *et cetera*. The boy doesn't sound Jersey at all, even though he is from Paterson, a few miles north of my stomping ground, Trenton. I've had a business there since I was eighteen, mostly contract work out of my home, and I do a good dollar.

If you want a life, you can get a life. This is what I've always told myself, anyway. So at thirty-six, I said, Gennine, just stop the madness and find a nice guy who isn't a serial killer.

That night, after the Captain Ahab Seafood Buffet, we go to a casino the size of a football field and done up like your typical Dodge City saloon. Two girls barely out of puberty say "Hi, there, partners" as they hand us cowboy hats and chaps. Matt fits the chaps over his grey striped Ralph Lauren trousers. It's a confusing fashion statement. He gazes across the brightly lit casino as four security guards haul a metal cart filled with grey canvas bags toward the teller's cage.

"Excuse me," Matthew says, adjusting the cowboy hat low on his forehead. "I'll just be a sec, darlin'."

"You're gonna get hat hair," I say.

He bends and kisses my lips gently, whispering, "The sacrifice we outlaws have to endure. Order me a Chivas."

A little uh-oh bell goes off. My new husband does that John Wayne saunter, disappearing into the crowd and the lights. I have what Daddy calls a protective nature. The urge to watch Matthew's back is strong. They've got similarities, Dad and Hubby—a real sweetness, a vulnerability, that male bravado hiding a softer core. Neither are inept, or ask for help easily, though what man does. Many a weekend I helped Daddy up the stairs, removed his shoes, watched as he gargled the beer stink from his breath, and tucked his skinny self under the sheet while Mommy slept quietly beside him. Perhaps Matt's that way, too.

69

I play electronic poker for an hour or so, card images rising beneath the glass table magically and with video game sound effects. Then I feel a kiss on my neck. I turn and stare at my cowboy husband in his Ralph Lauren and chaps. His face seems relaxed enough, but his eyes look crazy, or maybe crazy's the wrong word. The boy's pupils are vibrating. I've never seen a person's pupils do the vibrate thing; it's disconcerting. Matt swallows the Chivas I'd ordered for him in a single gulp. His eyes begin calming down.

7:40 AM, SUNDAY
THE JULIA ROBERTS HONEYMOON SUITE

While Matthew's in the shower singing a Marvin Gaye medley, I knock back two aspirins without water and stumble over to the closet. Reaching down for my suitcase, a black leather something appears. It's a small duffle bag. I try to remember if Matt brought this piece aboard the ship. After I open the draw strings, I have to switch on the light. Packs of hundred dollar bills stuff the bag like a bloated turkey. My God, there must be what, two hundred thousand? No, no, closer to three...I dunno...Jesus, probably a half million. The shower stops. Matt's still singing, "...what's goin' on...what's going on..." I shove the leather duffle bag into the far shadows of the closet, shut the door, and plop myself on the dishevelled bed.

Then from the closed bathroom, Matthew yells, "Hey!"

"Hey," I say back.

"This sea air really gets a person hungry." His voice stays slightly hurried and louder than necessary. "You hungry, sweetie? I'm starving, y' know? I could eat myself six, seven pancakes, maybe those link sausages. You think they got links? Maybe a few eggs, too. Yeah, a couple of sunny-side ups, y' know? What you think?"

I think you sound like a poster child for speed.

Matt says, "You there?"

"Uh-huh. Great, hon."

The Early Bird Breakfast Buffet has a long line. Most people are talking about food: the crisp bacon, the colourful red, orange, and pale green melon balls, the pancakes and link sausages, the scrambled eggs all fresh and fluffy nestled in their silver chaffing dishes. Listen carefully and you can hear passengers salivating. My new hubby, on the other hand, stares at the wedding ring of a slim, grey-haired woman three spaces up from us. Maybe Matthew doesn't dance to his own drummer, exactly, but at the very least, the boy sways.

He nods toward the ring, whispering to me, "How many carets, you figure?" Matt's wearing a white linen suit with tan Italian loafers and no socks. I can smell the Armani.

"Five, maybe six," I say, without hesitating.

Marriage should be based on compromise. Each of us brings old baggage to a relationship. Our success or failure with the other person can be measured on how well we manage that baggage. My girlfriend Ro says finding a good man is like looking for plutonium. Even if you find it, you've got a problem.

During the afternoon, as Matthew plays shuffle board with the elderly rich, I sneak down to our honeymoon suite to check the closet. The ring is in the black leather duffle bag, all right, wrapped inside a crumpled paper napkin that reeks of bacon. Okay, fine, give credit where it's due, the man's a professional. Things could be a lot worse. I could've married a drooling idiot who robs gas stations and has a poor fashion sense.

~

I must have fallen asleep last night before Matthew got to bed. Now he's in the shower doing his Smoky Robinson falsetto, and *way* too chirpy for this early hour. Curiosity has become my drug of choice. I actually tip-toe over to the closet like the Coyote sneaking up on the Roadrunner. Despite all efforts, I've become a Saturday morning cartoon. Worse, really, I see Matt as a well-dressed tooth fairy but with better presents.

Besides the money and the five or six caret diamond ring wrapped in a breakfast napkin, the black leather duffle bag now contains two ruby rings of an equally husky weight and a

71

choker of sapphires the size of babies' fingers surrounded by diamonds. It's the last item that takes my breath. My new hubby has the *cojones* to steal this necklace off Nicky C's personal bimbo. What's *wrong* with the boy? Even a plant knows you don't grow on Nicky C's side of the street.

Matt and my father are reflections of one another. I remember a June night and a monster of a guy beating Daddy in the front yard for cheating at a poker game. Picture a twelve year old leaping on the back of that thug—Mommy had locked herself inside the downstairs closet—and I'm wailing on his head, screaming help or police, possibly both, I don't know. Finally, though, this oversized moron shakes me off and runs.

"What're you doing?" Matt's standing behind me, a white towel tied about his waist, his arms crossed in front of him. A barely noticeable smile attempts to surface at the corners of his mouth.

I tell him he's in nose deep ca-ca. Though I appreciate his massive *cojones*, I tell him Nicky C will take those big boys and sauté them in butter. Matthew actually *laughs*. Hel-*lo*? Then he says how we're taking the bag to the bank tomorrow morning, when we make our Grand Cayman stop.

"How exactly does a person rob a casino in the middle of the Caribbean?" I want to know.

"You own the security guards," he says, doing both his John Wayne voice and saunter as he returns to the bathroom. Then, before closing the door, "You also exchange three very good bags of print for the real deal."

By the evening, having had a few glasses of pinot during and after dinner, I'm feeling far less ruffled about our situation. Now my new hubby and I are alone on the stern of deck two, leaning against the metal railing and watching a full moon go silver across the dark water. Matthew seems practically sane.

This serenity doesn't last. A large silhouette rises from one of the wood and canvas deck chairs. Nicky C steps into the moonlight, wearing a Hawaiian shirt, plaid Bermudas, and black wing-tips. The man's holding something that looks like a miniature howitzer. He's concerned about his sapphire and diamond necklace.

The first time I killed a person I'd just turned eighteen. I used my father's gun, an army .45 he kept in the nightstand by the bed. Daddy never tired of cheating dangerous men, and this particular thug had caught him in our driveway. I unloaded all seven shells into the man's head, though there wasn't much left of the guy after the first two. But you live and learn, refine your skills. Why use an entire clip when one properly aimed shell does the job?

That's what I do now.

I lift my Prada bag to chest level—a J Lo Glamour Girl Clutch—my hand reaching inside for the Berretta, and I fire one shot, the shell ripping through silk and sequins, hitting Nicky C in the forehead. It's like harpooning a grey whale, except quicker.

Matthew is staring at me, nodding, a smirk breaking to a wide open grin, letting me know, *Lady, I had your number right from the start*. Then the boy says, "So how long you been doin' that?"

Tossing the handbag and the Berretta overboard, I say, "Long enough." And dismiss the question with one of my own. "You gonna grab the guy's feet, or what?"

The Madman or, a Perfect Fit

Peter James McGuire

Peter McGuire is a senior year English and history student at the University of Colorado at Boulder. He has been previously published in the spring 2008 *Rose and Thorn* e-zine and is active in Denver's slam poetry scene.

I could hear the corpse rolling in the trunk of my car as I met another bend of the winding cliff road. The rain hitting the roof pounded out the rhythm of my heartbeat. The frozen leather of the steering wheel twisted in my shaking hands, the car unwilling to hold to the road, insisting it was too wet, too slippery, too fast, too late. I overpowered it, loving the sensation. It felt like the early days, when my father took me out on Sunday afternoons, when the suburban roads lay before me like bowed servants before a king. Only my father's prudence and the creeping Lincoln Continentals slowed my passage. I grinned as I sailed by them: a galleon leaving the dock in search of the new world.

"Wait 'til we reach the farms," my father murmured with a quiet but commanding tone.

But when the houses sank into the grain, everything faded but me and the horizon. The pounding of the engine killed all lingering thoughts of inferiority. I was in control. The wheel jittered with the irregularities of the asphalt: delicious.

The Madman's neck had felt the same as he had struggled for air. Writhing and protesting, he had screamed and clawed, but my grip had been too practiced and powerful. His head had become a red balloon as he fought.

"Why? Why? Why?" he had croaked over and over. The tears, the blood: crimson and clear into the blue rug below him. "Why?" *Why?*

I had spit in his face as he struggled. I had savoured the motion: the pumping of my heart, the twisting of the struggle, the joy of the revenge. Then all motion stopped.

I climbed out of the car and looked at the moon. Only about two hours left. I should have hurried, should have, but instead I stared at him, lying there in the trunk. He had bounced into the shovel during the drive and crushed his face on its broad side.

"Come, now. We mustn't dally," I whispered to him, savouring the wet sticking sound of the shovel dislodging from the cavity of his flattened face.

I took my time, slinging the Madman over my shoulder, plopping him down in the mud, propping him up so he could watch. His nose was crushed, teeth broken, jaw bent, but his eyes in his perfectly formed eye sockets remained. They shimmered blue in the moonlight. I stared at the grotesque mannequin I had created.

The ground gave easily as I dug, loosened by the rain. Every shovelful of dirt displaced filled almost instantly with mud. I dug faster.

It rained the day they buried my parents, too. The caskets were closed at the wake. We couldn't have all the finely constructed ladies in their new black dresses see what happens when two cars collide at ninety miles per hour, the jagged metal collapsing inwards on two fragile bodies. The mascara would have run, sure, but not for any tragedy other than the loss of a gossip partner. Let it be for the idea of grief, for what grievers are meant to look like.

Maybe it was best that I hadn't seen them in front of me. Maybe it was best that the only glimpse I had at their carnal wreckage was the night I broke into the police records. Maybe, but imagining the gore beneath the oak panels as they descended into that muddy hole sickened me.

The Madman's gaze belittled me as I dug his grave. I laughed at him. "I'm still your slave, aren't I? I slaved for you living and now I slave for you dead." I laughed again. His eyes seemed so dull, so empty. They were so bright and vivid, panicked and wild when my hands were around his neck. They were so tender and kind when he packed his children's lunches before driving them to school.

I tried to work my schedule around his at first, but I had to quit my job. I tried to understand him by following him. I tried to explain him to myself. I tried to become him, only to glean a little piece of mind from the idea that maybe he was deeply

77

flawed, maybe he was damaged, maybe he could be explained or excused. I followed him because I wanted to know that I was not him.

I wanted to know that I was not him.

Following him was better than my boring and pointless work. Each day I put on a tie. Each day I sat behind a computer, talking on a phone, making corporate sales, gleaning corporate profits from corporate consumers. I was so bored. I contemplated death constantly. I thought about freezing to death in the backyard, or in the park, or driving on the wrong side of the road, or drowning in the bathtub, or falling off the roof. I prayed that the house had a gas leak, or that a light switch would electrocute me, or that I would get in a car crash. I was bored.

The digging felt almost therapeutic, like meditation, or developing the rolls of film I used during the day. The repetitive action let my mind wander. But then I caught those eyes. I couldn't get them to close. The coroner couldn't get my mother's to, either, he told me as I played the part of grieving son. It suited me. It was like playing sick in elementary school. I didn't have to go to work for a week. I wore pyjamas and ate only soup. People came and went like marionettes in a clockwork show.

"How are you feeling," they demanded.

"Very sad and very alone," I replied flatly. *How am I feeling?*

"I thought that you didn't see your parents much after you went to college."

"Well I still loved them very much!" *Don't contradict me.*

"Well, I hope you feel better soon..." and they jumped on their planes.

How am I feeling?

I could grieve just as well at work, I discovered. I could grieve just as well in the bushes outside the Madman's house, I discovered. He came home in the middle of the day, sometimes, when his wife and kids were gone. Usually he'd just eat lunch and watch some TV before heading back to work, but sometimes he'd masturbate while hanging himself. I watched through the window, shocked the first time it happened, like watching a suspense movie. The more I watched him do it, the more I contemplated doing it myself. I never have, though.

I really haven't.

The meagre inheritance went to cameras and film, so, without a job, money became scarce. I ate Top Ramen at every meal. I had to sell the TV. The only entertainment came from inspecting the police report and accompanying photos I stole that night. The rest of my life atrophied like unused muscle. I had to sell the stereo. I started eating peanut butter sandwiches for variety. Friends stopped calling. Neighbours stopped visiting. The goldfish died.

The sides of the hole came up to my knees in most places now. *Maybe I'm burying myself more than I'm burying him*, I thought. *Maybe I'm sinking into the earth. Maybe it's eating me.* My boots were now completely full of mud and squelched as I walked around the pit. The Madman looked different in real life than he did in his mug shot. Normally people are dishevelled and angry in their mug shots, but he looked happy and well-rested; it was taken weeks after the crime, after he got out of the hospital. The state thought it would be cruel to arrest him while he was still convalescing. My father convalesced for three days before he died. My mother died at the scene.

I broke into the police records three weeks after the crash. I paid a janitor to let me in the back door and then got my money back by threatening to turn him in. Their folder was filed with the pending investigations. When I got home I read the report. And vomited.

I stalked him after that. I stalked him for three months. Assuming I only paid for food and gas, I could have carried on for another two.

The rain had almost stopped, now only falling sporadically. The ground was turning an unearthly greenish brown as the sun nudged up against the horizon. Things gained definition (where before they faded into the formless night): the car, the shovel, the grave, the Madman.

The report said that when he hit them, he was on the wrong side of the road. He was driving on the wrong side of the winding cliff road. I cried violently when I read it. All the hours I fantasized about driving on the wrong side of the road, clicking aimlessly in my cubicle. All the hours I dreamed of getting hit by an innocent driver on the right side. All the hours I dreamed not of dying, but of coming close. All the hours I spent bored.

Life is boring. I prayed every night that there was another reason, but after three months of following him, no other explanation presented itself. They died because he was bored.

I was bored. The only relief was the few months I spent following the Madman, following his routine instead of living mine. The only relief.

The grave was finished. My brain seized up like a rusted clock. The endpoint was here. *Put him in the grave. Fill the grave with dirt. Drive away. The end. The end?*

I put the Madman in the grave. He looked so small and lonely. It was slightly too tall for him, and way too wide. I took off my boots. It was wide enough for two. I lay down beside him. Dirt lightly caressed the top of my head and the balls of my feet. His arm touched mine lightly. I closed my eyes. It was a perfect fit.

Vendetta

Suzzanne Myers

Suzzanne can't remember when she started writing. She was ten when her dad let her borrow his typewriter on which to work. That was all it took—that and a lot of paper. She was inspired by Frank Herbert's vision of humanity, by Louis L'Amour's old-fashioned heroic romance, by Wilbur Smith's far-reaching, gritty adventures. Now, many years later, she is living in the Pacific Northwest with her husband and an African Grey parrot who thinks that creative genius is found somewhere deep within her ear.

Suzzanne is focused on writing stories about the human condition set within an historical or fantasy context and she strives for unique perspectives that make the reader think every step of the way. She is also a member of the online writing group Quill-Thrill.Com where she works with other aspiring writers to hone their talent and keep the creative process flowing. She has always found the dark hero or the anti-hero a fascinating character full of potential.

The letter was a plea.

The assassin, Kyaltos Aremis had said, was nothing if not an educated man. Could be nothing if there was nothing within him, could take nothing if he didn't comprehend the value of his procurement. He read the written works of men so that he might know them as they knew themselves, for it was in the written word, Kyaltos taught, that a man's heart was revealed. The cant of his lettering, the depth of ink, even the very words he chose—different in any other language—could describe the avenues of his soul. This, then, was a goal of the trained Cyprian: to script—that is, to read a man in his words, to know him by them, to understand who he was and what his life had been. Only then could he discover how to plot the man's death.

Khuamen had known these things, had also been a pupil under Master Aremis once. But that was a long time ago, when he went by a Theban name, when he was not a king. The moment Telcinus set foot on Egyptian soil, Khuamen knew why he was there. He was old now and wise enough to realize that Telcinus would not be stopped, not with a thousand spies and all the palace guard turned out to find him. Instead, Khuamen had sent only the plea.

A king should have been more careful, Telcinus thought.

I am your friend, the letter said. Nothing more than that. But the letters were broad and quickly drawn, the ink a light, uncertain stain. *Trust me*, it seemed to say, and perhaps, *forget the past*.

But it was impossible for Telcinus not to remember what had happened all those years ago. To think of the boy he'd been, a loving, trusting boy, beholden to the man who'd owned him, who'd called himself *father* instead of *master*. And then

82

how he'd learned the worth of a slave, when he was bound upon an altar, a sacrifice to make a foreign people believe a Theban should be their living god. Left hopeless and destroyed upon that altar by the man's greed, with all that he was and could've been hollowed out and cast away like so much rubbish.

Forget the past. Or was it, *forgive me*?

They were words he'd longed to hear, words that even now made his willpower falter. He had loved the man who became Khuamen. But those words were not the truth behind the plea. The only thing that had ever been in Khuamen's heart was a hunger for power. Never remorse. He'd coveted the wife of the old Egyptian king, had murdered him, had then sacrificed an innocent boy to assure the people that the gods favoured his coup, had even forced his new wife to hold the dagger. If her heart had been as cold as his she might have cut the boy's neck a little deeper. For that kindness, Telcinus did not hate her.

But forgiving Khuamen was something he could not do.

Telcinus knew a rational man couldn't live his life in the past. It was something he'd learned in the years since, but even so, he could not deny that he was a result of that past, a product of the wrong that had been done to him. He'd hoped never to see Khuamen again, had thought that if he stayed away he could erase the man's memory altogether. And he had almost done it, had almost forgotten so many, many times.

But the past was vivid and real now. It was a girl kneeling on a temple floor, the princess Merekhet, Khuamen's only heir. It was a scar to mark how he'd survived, that he could never truly forget. And it was a Cyprian gift; final acknowledgement of the vendetta that brought him to the Brotherhood long ago. He'd made his choice back then and now it had led him back. Now it would be done.

The ink shaped and reformed in his mind, stretched out across the paper, reached for him. Khuamen's voice pleaded, *don't kill her*.

The girl's eyes flickered, looked up at him briefly. They were sharp Egyptian eyes, fired with amber irises, and he did not think they missed much. "I knew you were here."

A usurper should have known better, Telcinus thought, as he drew the dagger from his sleeve. The grip was familiar in his hand, comforting. Khuamen should never have revealed so much. "Then you know the time has come."

Merekhet kissed the feet of the great statue before which she knelt. It was carved in the likeness of a woman with a lioness's head and it bore a fierce scowl. The girl dipped two fingers in a bowl of oil to anoint the stone and looked back at him. "Does it have to be this way?"

He read the uncertainty on her face, saw apprehension and hard decision commingled in her yellow eyes, found himself admiring that much about her. He said only, "It's the choice you made."

"Yes," she sighed. "Did you know I asked them to send you?" She studied him, tracing the line of the old scar that ran from his ear to the hollow at his throat. It was white and long ago healed, but her gaze made it ache anew. "My mother died when I was still very young, but she wrote of you, of a man with a scar like yours. And she wrote of my true father. I wanted it to be you."

So the girl understood that much of the events that had shaped her life. It struck him suddenly that he was the only one privy to these last moments of her innocence, while she hesitated to take that final step and cross a threshold from which she could never come back. It seemed a strange thing that he should find this moment memorable, that he would feel such a strong desire now to prolong it as long as possible, but he remembered it had been the same for him when he fell on his knees before the Brotherhood and swore Death's Oath.

Was it compassion he felt now? Or was it what the rapist felt as he held his victim close and savoured her virtue, knowing that once had, it was forever lost? Had the girl's mother felt like this when she held the dagger to his skin, he wondered? He remembered her eyes, narrow and pretty like her daughter's. Afraid. Had she realized she would destroy him then? Had she cherished the moment before she did it? Had she remembered it again at her own end?

Merekhet reached up and took his hand, pulled him down to squat in front of her. "Pretend that we are just a man and woman, nothing more. What would you say then? Would it have to be like this?"

He stared at the ripples of white linen that pooled around her legs, at the cream-colored soles of her feet, at the slender, graceful fingers that had interlocked with his and only just then released, seeming to realize they'd trespassed by touching him.

He did not rub his fingertips together, but the feel of her skin lingered on them all the same. *If I were only a man*, he thought.

But he said, "We are never just men and women. We never can be."

"Then what are we?"

He leaned forward, watching her eyes shift back and forth. "Shades. Of what we should have been."

Merekhet smiled, but it was bittersweet. Then she reached out and laid her fingers against the foot of her stone goddess. "Sometimes I think I am meant only to be a toy for the rest of the world to play with." She looked up into the lioness's stern visage. "I want to be more than that."

"Then it's up to you to be more." He licked his lips. "Are you afraid?"

"No." Her shoulders fell and she sat back against the wall behind her. The slender muscles in her neck shifted as she turned to watch a servant lighting a censer across the hall. "It's what I've known I would do all my life. But I wish you would've turned down the offer."

What could he say to her? How could he explain the tumult of his life, that he was still a boy, still trapped under the knife of her mother? That this was the culmination of years of work even as he tried to forget what drove him to do it? That when she'd sent to the Brotherhood, he'd known exactly what he must do?

He could stop it. He could turn and leave with not another word despite how it would stay with him the rest of his days. The girl would send for another, eventually. He knew it, had recognized that much about her even if she didn't know it about herself yet. But at least then Telcinus could say he had not been the one to take her innocence from her.

85

"That was *my* choice to make," he said simply, and understood that he could not leave, not even if she commanded him to. Death was what Khuamen had taught him and he'd learned the lesson well. He'd made his choice.

There were footsteps in the hall outside. The sound of bronze and leather. A man's voice calling her name.

"I regret it," she whispered. "You might have forgotten this, some day." She looked up at him and in her eyes he saw his own pain. Saw tears there, and remorse. "Who would you have been?"

"Not a slave," he whispered. He leaned forward. "There is no redemption for me, lady. Not in this, not ever. What I've done to come this far cannot be forgiven."

She shook her head. "I know. But I will remember you."

He nodded, accepting that. "Remember your part as well." He rose and slid up behind the statue of the lioness even as twenty of the king's guard poured into the hall, fanning out around their master. Khuamen saw Merekhet sitting alone against the base of the statue and cried out, running toward her.

I am your friend, the letter said. And Telcinus had sent his reply back, saying only, *You will find her in the temple hall.*

A man who knew the Brotherhood should have been suspicious, should have recognized the subtlety of the words, the promise couched in each short, quick stroke. A usurper should have realized his mistake, that his daughter was never in any danger. Should not have come, even with a hundred guardsmen.

But an old man loved his child. Even if she was not truly his, even if she secretly hated him for the real father he'd stolen from her. Another ten years and old age might've given Merekhet the throne she deserved. But it was not a kingdom she wanted, not a throne that had brought her to this moment. She sat up amidst the ripples of white linen, smiled at the man who'd called himself her father, reached out her hand. If Khuamen had known what lay in the heart of his daughter, he might not have loved her. Might not have been blinded by it. But he did not suspect it, having fallen in love with her beguiling smile, her gentle beauty. His face lit with joy to see

86

her still alive and he laughed as he ran to grab her up in his arms.

Telcinus lamented that the innocence he'd cherished in her was now gone, as he came around the back side of the statue and caught the usurper's topknot in his grasp. He set the sharpened bronze against Khuamen's neck beneath the statue of a lion-headed goddess.

He looked up and saw it in Merekhet's eyes, those fierce amber eyes. She knew the cost of what had been done, understood too that redemption was not hers to give. The blood was already pumping beneath his knife. There was a gurgle in Khuamen's throat and his frail limbs flailed wildly. There could be no going back now; she'd made her choice. They were across the threshold and here, now, there was only acknowledgement between killers, between those who would not be slaves, who would never forget. At the last, they understood each other. Telcinus smiled, inclined his head even as he heard the angry howl of the guardsmen behind him, heard their swords torn free from their scabbards. She could not save him, but it was well made, this end.

A king was dead. In his place, his daughter lived, and remembered.

The Mouse King

S.C. Hayden

S.C. Hayden is a 34-year-old registered nurse, living, working, and writing in Savannah, Georgia. His fiction has appeared or is forthcoming in a number of small press journals and magazines in the US and CA including: *All Hallows*, *The Dirty Goat*, *M Brane SF*, *Mecrography*, and *Portland Review*. Visit www.schayden.com for more on S.C. Hayden.

Today, The Mouse King thought, *is going to be a good day.* Sunshine dappled the tree-lined sidewalk. Paper cups and cigarette buts, caught in the morning breeze, skittered lightly across the pavement. The city seemed somehow calmed, steeped in the soft spring sun; its usual garish countenance had softened. It was beautiful, sublime, and in an instant, the tranquil image imploded.

Directly beside him, a light blue Buick erupted into sound. Inside the Buick, a fat, flushed, fleshy-faced man was laying on his horn. The traffic, of course, was at a standstill. *The traffic*, The Mouse King thought, *is always at a standstill at eight o'clock on a Monday morning.* Blasting the horn wasn't going to solve anything. So rare, these moments of peace, and it was all being ruined by one fat-faced asshole in a Buick.

In an instant, The Mouse King's blood was boiling. He stopped, clutched the aluminium post of a No Parking sign and closed his eyes. The Mouse King imagined pounding a metal railroad spike through the fat man's head with a steel mallet. The image was sharp and clear. He could hear the clank of metal on metal as he drove the spike home. He imagined himself slicing the man's cheeks open with a razor blade, imagined ripping out the fat bastard's tongue and eating it. Slowly, The Mouse King relaxed.

Moments after he'd started walking again, a young woman pushed a stroller directly across his path. The Mouse King stopped short mid stride and nearly fell over. The woman walked on, pushing the stroller with one hand and holding a cell phone pressed against her head with the other, oblivious.

The Mouse King squeezed his eyes shut and clenched his fists. He wanted to snatch the stroller away from the ditsy young mother and push it into the street. He pressed his palms against his eyelids. Tiny lights flickered in the darkness. The Mouse King swayed. *If I don't calm down*, he thought, *I'm going to pass out.*

By the time he'd reached the bus stop, his pleasant mood had transmuted entirely. When the Number Seven arrived, The Mouse King got on and took a seat between an obese woman with plastic curlers in her hair, and a pimply young man bathed in nauseating, cheap cologne. With tremendous effort, The Mouse King steadied his trembling hands and removed a book from his knapsack.

The Mouse King had read *Torture Devices of the Spanish Inquisition* in its entirety countless times, and still shuddered with the same giddy excitement whenever he opened it. He felt the beginnings of an erection as he thumbed through the well-worn pages and studied the various diagrams and illustrations. Some of the devices depicted were elaborate contraptions of wood and iron, replete with wheels, pulleys, and levers, designed to crush bones and rend flesh, while others, like the infamous Judas Cradle, were simple, elegant, and beautifully brutal in form and function. But there was one device The Mouse King loved above all others. It was called, simply, a Pear.

It was a small, pear-shaped cylinder, with a long screw on one end. The inquisitor placed the base of the Pear into the subject's mouth. As the screw was turned, the Pear would open wider and wider until the subject's mouth was stretched far beyond its natural limit, until the flesh tore and the jaw bone dislocated, if that was what was wanted, and *that*, The Mouse King suspected, was exactly what was wanted. Of course, the mouth was not the only place a Pear could be inserted. The inquisitor would insert the Pear into the offending orifice: the mouth for heretics, the rectum for sodomites, and the vagina for unchaste women.

The Mouse King looked up from his book. In the seat directly in front of him, a woman was breast-feeding her baby. She wasn't even attempting to be discreet about it. God, how he hated that. She held her child with one arm, cradling its head

91

with her hand, half of her swollen tit plainly visible. With her free hand, she held a magazine. Everyone on the bus could see her exposed boob and she didn't even care. She was reading a magazine for God's sake!

In a perfect world, The Mouse King thought, *as punishment for her incredible immodesty, she would be forced to breast-feed baby crocodiles.* He pictured a pair of little crocks snapping at her nipples, mangling her breast with their tiny, needle-sharp teeth. He imagined her forced to do this before a crowd of strangers who laughed and jeered and placed bets as to which crock would be first to chew off a nipple. The Mouse King laughed out loud. The woman glanced up from her magazine with an uneasy expression and pressed her baby tight against her chest.

When at last, The Mouse King was at work, sitting snugly in his cubical, he began to relax. The Mouse King enjoyed his work. All day long he spoke on the telephone with people he had never met and would likely never meet. He entered the homes of strangers, sometimes hundreds of miles away, through the telephone—heard their voices, their breath. He read their profiles on his computer screen: name, address, current long distance carrier. He didn't even have to dial the phone; the computer did it for him. He waited for someone to answer, then asked if Mr. or Mrs. So-And-So was present, and if they would like to save money on their long distance telephone calls.

Everyone responded differently. Some were polite, some were rude, some were outright hostile, shouting profanities and denunciations of every ilk. Some hung up after only a few words, while others prattled on endlessly about all kinds of silly things. Once, a woman, in a breathy whisper, asked him what he was wearing. The Mouse King listened to them all, noting the inflections of their voices, their patterns of speech. He tried to guess what they looked like, the lives they lived, what they loved, what they feared. And all the while, as they discussed the potential benefits of changing long distance carriers, he imagined ways he would torture them.

The name Anne Berkovitz appeared on his screen. Anne, his computer terminal informed him, lived at 35 Oakview Terrace in Brookline, Massachusetts, and was a customer of AT&T. The Mouse King hit the Enter key on his keyboard, and his computer dialled the number. After a quick series of clicks and beeps, Anne's telephone rang, seven hundred miles away.

"Hello," an older woman's voice spoke in The Mouse King's ear.

"May I speak with Anne Berkovitz, please?"

"Speaking," the woman said.

"Would you be interested in saving money on your long distance telephone calls?"

"I'm sorry, but I don't speak to telemarketers."

Your name tells me that you are a Jewess, and what is that hint of accent? Polish? German? Your voice places you in your mid seventies. Do you have a set of numbers tattooed across your wrist? Do you still have nightmares? Does the sound of a siren make you tremble, even though you know it to be nothing more than an ambulance passing in the night? Do men in uniform make you uneasy? I could rekindle those fears for you, Anne, I could make them live and breathe again.

"I apologize for the intrusion, Mrs. Berkovitz, but it will only take a moment. This is a very important offer…"

Usually, when The Mouse King finished his shift, he would volunteer to put in a few extra hours, but today was a special day, and The Mouse King was impatient. He glanced up at the clock every fifteen minutes or so, trying to will the time faster, but the minutes dragged regardless. At five o'clock, The Mouse king leaped from his cubical and hurried to the door.

What people don't understand, The Mouse King thought, *is how ignorant we were during the Inquisition. With only a rudimentary knowledge of the mechanics of pain, how much, realistically, could be accomplished?* What The Mouse King wanted, more than anything in the world, wasn't to be transported back to the time of the Inquisition, but that the Inquisition could happen *today. Imagine it*, he thought, *imagine what could be done with today's technology, with today's understanding of human psychology, with modern pharmaceuticals, with modern surgical technique!*

93

What a grand inquisitor The Mouse King would make. To such great heights he would bring the craft of torture. Only the greatest minds in history would rival his artistry: Beethoven, DaVinci, Stalin. What a shame it was, what a testament to the hopelessness of our times that a man of his particular genius, of his unique gift, was forced to work with mice.

When The Mouse King opened the door of his one-room apartment, Miss Trixie leapt from the threadbare sofa and trotted across the floor to meet him. "Hello Miss Trixie," The Mouse King said. "Were you good? Did you miss me? Are you hungry?" Miss Trixie's yellow eyes stared up at him. Her pupils momentarily contracted into a pair of thin, dark slits before dilating slowly, waxing black blades in pools of yellow-green. She blinked lazily and rubbed the length of her body across his lower calf. "Well, Miss Trixie, tonight's the big night, isn't it?" The Mouse King said, and walked into the apartment.

Weeks earlier, The Mouse King had placed an ad on an Internet dating site that catered to *special* interests.

Submissive male seeks female dominatrix, for light punishment and humiliation. This is my first time, so please be experienced. I want to learn. Serious replies only.

To which he received the following reply:

I am an experienced dominatrix, willing to teach. I come highly recommended and my technique is impeccable. My price, 200 dollars per hour, is non-negotiable. No one has ever been disappointed.

After a brief period of communication, during which methods and ground rules were discussed, a time and date were agreed upon. That night at eight pm, Clemency, as she so cryptically called herself, would be arriving. The Mouse King fluttered about his apartment in anticipation. He was so giddy that he decided to forgo all of his experiments for the rest of the day.

The Mouse King's experiments were in evidence all around him. Small, wire mesh cages filled the apartment. There were hundreds of them. Cages lined the walls, cages sat on kitchen counters, cages were stacked on top of cages, and all of them were filled with white mice.

The Mouse King squatted beside a plastic bucket filled with water and peered over the rim. A small white mouse paddled around inside in an endless circle, struggling to keep its head above water. A quarter ounce lead fishing weight was attached to one of the mouse's hind legs with a rubber band. The Mouse King wanted to see how long it would take the mouse to drown. He had placed the mouse in the bucket that morning before leaving for work, and there it was, still going strong. It was part of an ongoing experiment. He wanted to know exactly how long the mouse could last, so he could remove the next subject from the bucket in the last moment before it died, only to place it in again, after an hour's rest. For torture to be successful, it must be prolonged as long as possible.

Beside the bucket, there was a cardboard box. The Mouse King looked inside and grinned delightedly. Over the years, The Mouse King had electrocuted, suffocated, disembowelled, impaled, and incinerated thousands of mice, but starvation experiments were his favourite. Three days earlier, he'd cemented a mouse's hind legs in a plaster mould, dropped it in the box, and placed some food just out of reach. The mouse had actually chewed through its own legs to free itself from the plaster and reach the food. The tiny creature slither-crawled, smearing blood about the inside of the box as it dragged its mangled legs.

At exactly eight pm, the door buzzer sounded. The Mouse King's heart fluttered in his chest. He took a second to smooth his hair with his open palms before sprinting to the door. Looking through the keyhole, he saw nothing but cleavage, pale white breasts sequestered in a black leather corset. He opened the door as quickly as he could, trying, with only limited success, to steady his trembling hands. When the door was opened, The Mouse King's breath caught in his throat. Elegant yet powerful, she stood a full head and shoulders above him. Ebony hair and snow-white skin, wrapped in glossy black leather. He felt that he was gazing at a pagan goddess.

"Aren't you going to invite me in, Mr. Pranks?"

The Mouse King blinked for a moment, not sure who she meant, then remembered that he'd used the name "Buster Pranks" as his online pseudonym.

"Yes, yes of course, come in," he stammered.

Clemency carried a small wooden chair with a circular hole cut in the seat, and a black leather bag. When she was inside of what passed as The Mouse King's living room, she looked cautiously about herself, taking in the scene of clutter and disarray. The room reeked of animal stink and singed hair. There was hardly space to walk, let alone set down the chair and conduct a proper session. The Mouse King scurried about, clearing buckets, cages, and power tools from the centre of the room.

"Please forgive the mess," The Mouse King said, spreading a stained bath towel over a metal box attached to a car battery. "It's just that I've been so busy, I scarcely have time to clean. You see, I'm something of a scientist."

Clemency glanced at a knee-high coffee table in the corner of the room. A small white mouse was pinned, through its limbs, to the tabletop. The mouse panted rapidly, its body twitched rhythmically, its tail twisted and slithered back and forth like a wounded snake. Tiny drops of blood coated the fine white hairs around its delicate muzzle.

"A scientist?" she asked.

"Oh, yes," The Mouse King went on enthusiastically, completely missing the distaste in the tall woman's voice. "I conduct all kinds of important research. One day I hope to take my work to a higher level, but that's another topic entirely."

"I see."

When an adequate space had been cleared, Clemency set the chair down and dropped her black leather bag to the floor. The bag hit the hardwood floor with a metallic clank. The Mouse King jumped at the sound.

"Take off all of your clothes and sit in the chair," she said, her face devoid of any trace of emotion. "From this point forward you will refer to me as Mistress, and you will speak only when spoken to. Is that understood?"

"Yes, Mistress," The Mouse King stammered.

As he undressed, The Mouse King kept his eyes closed. It was easier that way. Apart from a fumbled attempt at intimacy, ending in premature ejaculation and humiliation in the back seat of a Chevrolet during his last year in high school, The Mouse King had never been with a woman. Even with his eyes closed, he could feel her scrutiny boring into his flesh, reading his insecurities, analyzing his fear. Despite his efforts at self-control, he felt a stirring in his groin. This was what he wanted, what he needed: the humiliation, the shame. *At last*, he thought, *this is it!*

When The Mouse King was seated in the chair, his ass hanging through the hole in the seat, Clemency affixed his arms and legs securely to the chair's frame with long leather straps. Tightly bound and unable to free himself, a feeling of calmness and security settled over The Mouse King's being. Clemency, stately and regal in her leather corset, skirt, and boots, seemed at once both puissant and maternal.

Without speaking or any change in countenance, she undressed herself, unhooking buttons one by one. With her corset and skirt cast to the floor beside her, tall and beautiful, Clemency stood before The Mouse King, legs apart, hands on her hips. The letters P E T A were tattooed in black ink across her lower abdomen. She removed a roll of electrical tape from her bag, loosened a section, and covered The Mouse King's mouth.

All at once, his feelings of warmth and security vanished. *What is she doing?* he wondered. This didn't seem right. They were supposed to have a *safe* word. They had worked that out online. The safe word was *cupcakes*. What if she went too fast? What if he couldn't handle it? How was he going to say the safe word with his mouth taped shut? Sweat stood out on The Mouse King's back and forehead.

"You see, Mr. Pranks," Clemency said, "the beauty of the relationship between a dominatrix and a submissive is that the submissive *wants* to be punished. The submissive is a consenting partner. That consent, Mr. Pranks, is what separates what I do, from what you do." She circled the chair as she spoke, letting her hand fall gently on his shoulder, her high-heeled boots clip-clopping on the hardwood floor. When she was in front of him again, she knelt down slowly beside her open black leather bag. "These mice are not consenting. They didn't ask to be tortured. They are not willing partners in your so-called experiments." Her dark eyes flashed as she spoke. "Since the mice are unable to speak for themselves," Clemency continued, "I'll speak for them."

She removed several items from her bag and laid them out on the floor beside her. A straight razor, a hammer, a hypodermic needle, a pair of pliers... She removed one last item and held it up to the light. A pear-shaped metal cylinder flashed in her hands.

"During the Spanish inquisition," Clemency whispered, "this object was known as a Pear."

Micro-Fiction Interlude

Authors were given the chance to submit works of micro-fiction exactly fifty words long. It's not an easy feat to encapsulate the essence of a story in so little space, but I believe the following five authors have succeeded beautifully. So why not join us in a brief interlude to witness life, and death, in a lightning flash—snapshot prose—of assassins in action.

My target goes down, I head home.
I find Janet dead, hear Mikey crying.
A shot kneecaps me, shooter is low.
"Mikey!" I hiss, "hide!"
I take one in the chest. It's Mikey with my Glock.
"Should've gotten me the Wii, Daddy…"
He doesn't waver, just aims.
I'm so prou…

Mark Onspaugh

Mark Onspaugh is a native Californian who grew up on a steady diet of horror, science fiction, and DC Comics. A proud member of the HWA, he writes screenplays, short stories, and novels. He was also one of the writers of the cult movie favourite *Flight of the Living Dead*. He lives in Los Osos, California, with his wife, author/artist Dr. Tobey Crockett. He can be found online at www.markonspaugh.com

A Death

He held his breath tighter than the knife he grasped. His goal: a young king's death. Like a tree, the boy would be felled. Before he could throw—a noise. He listened intently, trying to hear. Never did he blink or lose poise. He fell, servant's knife in his ear.

Zachary Thede

Zachary lives in Wisconsin and has been writing seriously for the last three years. He prefers writing fantasy but has also ventured into the realm of sci-fi.

Monday, the Water

Tuesday, the call.

"You've lost. Understand?"

Mary did. "Yes."

Click.

Wednesday and Thursday Mary didn't answer, but Friday she did.

"Payment?"

She shuddered. "Not yet."

Click.

Saturday, James was sweet, blue eyes beautiful as always. They kissed, Mary's face fragile, cracking.

Sunday she answered, holding two orbs of lovely blue.

Camille Alexa

Camille Alexa lives in an Edwardian home painted a hundred shades of white. Her work has appeared in *ChiZine*, *Fantasy Magazine*, and *Escape Pod*. A collection of her short fiction and poetry, *Push of the Sky*, is available from Hadley Rille Books. More information and an updated bibliography are available at www.camillealexa.wordpress.com

It was perfectly set. Ashley heard the spring release and time slowed to a crawl. She watched the line slacken, gears turning behind an ivy wall, perfectly hidden. She'd been setting these for years. As the trap door behind her slammed shut, she wished that she'd have set this one.

G. Elmer Munson

G. Elmer Munson is a New England writer who writes about the strange and unusual, as well as the horrors of everyday life. He lives with his family and many, many animals in a big old farmhouse where the night-time creaks and groans provide a seemingly unlimited source of inspiration. His work can be found in *DemonMinds*, *The Monsters Next Door* Issue 5 and "Best Of" print anthology *For the Love of Monsters*, and *Flash Scribe*.

The Idea Assassin

She murdered in flourishes: grey-haired, invisible in black, a rainbow-beaded lanyard swinging bifocals with deadly grace. In one hand: a red fountain pen to draw blood.

Poorly researched and thought out. See me after class.
C-

She licked the pen's red nib and threw the carcass to the floor.

Yvonne Pronovost

Yvonne Pronovost's fiction can be found on the pages of *NFG*, *Neo-Opsis Science Fiction Magazine*, and *Beyond Centauri* magazine. She has also appeared in several anthologies, including *A Field Guide to Surreal Botany* by Two Cranes Press, *Darkness Rising 2005* by Prime Books, and *Tesseracts Ten*, which was nominated for an Aurora Award. She currently lives in Edmonton, Canada, and volunteers as an administrative assistant for *Flash Me Magazine*.

We now return you to your regularly
scheduled murders.

The Man from Health and Safety

Michael Amos

Michael lives with his family in Oxfordshire, where he divides his time between the IT industry and writing. He has written articles for a variety of newspapers, magazines, and web sites, on subjects as diverse as woolly mammoths and belly-dancing. He has published two novels (*Homeland* and *The Rocktastic Corduroy Peach*) with Samhain Publishing Ltd. More information, and excerpts from his novels, is available at his website, www.michaelamos.net.

I) JUSSI BJORLING AND ROBERT MERRILL SINGING "THE PEARL FISHER'S DUET",
FROM BIZET'S *PEARL FISHERS*

"I'm sorry, buddy, the whole situation is more complicated than I was led to believe. She's dead."

Enrico closed his eyes. Elbows on the console, he massaged his temples while Alex, the man who masqueraded as his boss, continued talking on the video screen.

"I don't know how mission control managed to omit the fatality from the accident report. You'll have to find out what the hell they're playing at. I'm sorry. I know this isn't a good time for you."

A harmonious unison of voices sang "The Pearl Fisher's Duet" quietly in the tiny headphones lodged in Enrico's ears. The beauty and purity of this private music, it was his escape, his refuge, his release. Opening his eyes, he stared blearily at Alex. A response would be pointless. The distance back to Earth from Mars meant twenty minutes would elapse before Alex heard it.

Alex continued. "I haven't got anything more on the Oberon case. I've said it before; I can't see any grounds for them to prosecute you. We'll just have to see how it plays out. Anyway, send me a message when you touch down. Ciao."

The screen faded to a dark blue. Straightening up, Enrico switched it off.

Now they let him know there was a fatality! A month out from Earth, about to land on the Martian base, and now they let him know this open-shut case is in fact two month's solid paperwork.

Did they think he wanted to be sent on this job while Katelyn, dear, sweet, darling Katelyn, filed for divorce? Did he want to be here with the Oberon incident hanging over him?

"*Merda.*"

He took consolation in the private aria playing in his ears until the shuttle jolted, bringing him rudely back to the present. They had landed. The luxury of gravity came as a relief after four weeks of weightlessness. Mars's gravity was barely forty percent that of Earth's, but forty percent was better than nothing.

The mothership's super-efficient methane engine had brought him here at nearly half a million kilometres an hour. If he had his investigation and report sorted within a week, he could be on the mothership as it returned home. But a report within a week? When there had been a fatality?

"*Merda.*"

The door hissed open and a woman stuck her head through. Doe-brown eyes peeped shyly out at him from beneath the glossy black hair falling around her face. "Enrico Mancini, from Health and Safety?"

"Sì. Yes." Enrico smiled at her warmly. It was the sort of smile that had led Katelyn to the services of a lawyer.

The woman stepped into the room, extending a hand. "Hi, I'm Lucy Fullick, Spirituality Officer." She was English. Enrico loved English girls.

He shook her hand, firmly. "Enchanted."

"Ooh, a pleasure." She giggled, blushing as she extracted her hand. "If you'll come with me, I'll take you to your quarters so you can freshen up before you meet the commander."

"No, please. It's alright. Take me to see the commander straight away. Her name is Andrine Hucknell, yes?"

"Yes, that's her. Come on, then."

Lucy led him from the communications room and into the exit tunnel connecting the shuttle to the Martian base. Their steps were odd half-bounds.

Enrico watched the slow-motion rebound of Lucy's hair as she walked. She was fascinating. Worth pursuing. He didn't care about Katelyn. Why should he? He was as good as free now. "Have the clever *professores* found little green men yet?"

"No. Of course not."

"But that is the whole point of the mission?"

"Well, by necessity, this phase is, yes. In another three months, all this nonsense will be over. The mining companies will be allowed to come here and do something that is actually useful."

"You don't think they will find life, no?"

"The teachings of the International Church of the Reformed Testament are very clear on this. The Divinity created life on Earth alone. We are unique in the universe. There is no life to find."

Enrico smiled. As mission spirituality officer, Lucy no doubt believed the teachings of the International Church of the Reformed Testament, the ICRT, to the letter. It was a wise course. Questioning the ICRT's dictums, as many scientists and civil rights lawyers had done, led to an existence best described as uncomfortable. The Theocratic States of America stood for freedom, democracy, and the rule of law. With blasphemy on the statute books, scientists had to tread very carefully.

Lucy sighed. "I feel sorry for them. Anyone with any sense can see it is a clear waste of time. The world was created at nine in the morning on the twenty-third of October, four thousand and four years B.C. It's in the scriptures. All this NASA talk of Mars's environment being different a billion years ago is clearly nonsense. It didn't exist a billion years ago."

"I know nothing about these things. These are questions for bigger men than me. I do Health and Safety," Enrico said.

They were halfway down the exit tunnel by then. Lucy stopped and turned to him. Her frown was so childishly earnest that Enrico had to stifle a laugh. "These things are important, Enrico. Really, they are. There are a number of scientists, including some from NASA, who've written to Congress insisting that evolution be taught alongside Intelligent Design in schools. We cannot let this happen. It is immoral."

Enrico sighed. "Ms. Fullick, my job has taught me one thing over the years. The truth will always come out."

She smiled and looked down. "Yes, it will. But I do feel sorry for these silly scientists. They should use their cleverness to do something useful. Come on, this is something you don't see every day."

She took him to the threshold of the tunnel and they looked out at the interior of the Martian base, a huge circular biome of clear polymer hexagons supported by a steel frame. A cluster of small buildings at the centre was surrounded by a low growth of young pine trees, the tallest no more than three metres high. Overhead, lamps shone down to enhance the weak sunlight. Beyond the walls of the biome the red Martian desert stretched away to the horizon.

Lucy turned to him and grinned. "Welcome to Mars."

2) ROSA PONSELLE SINGING "HABANERA",
FROM BIZET'S *CARMEN*

"Enrico. Come in, please." Commander Andrine Hucknell was a large woman, her ruddy face capped with a mop of faded ginger curls.

Stepping into her office, Enrico shook her hand. "Commander Hucknell, I am pleased to make your acquaintance."

"Please, call me Andrine. Have a seat." As Enrico lowered himself into a chair, she produced a miniature bottle of whiskey and two small tumblers. "Care for one?"

A whiskey! His heart leapt. "Sì."

"I totally expect to have to resign, you understand?" Andrine handed over a generous glass. "As commander, the buck stops with me."

Enrico savoured a long sip, the warmth of the whiskey spreading amiably down his chest. The austere rules on the mothership had enforced a month's abstinence. In his ears, Rosa Ponselle delivered Bizet's aria like an angel: *L'amour est un oiseau rebelle que nul ne peut apprivoiser*—Love is a rebellious bird that nobody can tame. The melody washed over him.

"Enrico?"

"My pardon. Resign? Ah, no, we will see. I need to investigate all the circumstances."

"I appreciate that. Really I do. But Terri—Professor Terri Dawkins—the woman who died..."

"Sì."

"Well, she made the request to go out alone and that's against all the rules. I didn't check and I let her go."

"And then, what happened?"

"The fabric on the spacesuit had nearly worn through at the neck. She got a puncture a couple of miles out and suffocated. If she'd had a buddy with her, well, she might have stood a better chance."

"Okay, so the fabric of the suit had worn through. That is very bad. I would like to see the professor's body."

"Ah, no, that's not possible. She's already been frozen and her casket sealed up. There's a full death cert and autopsy report, though."

Enrico clicked his tongue for a few moments. "The suits are all the same design?"

"Yes, but there's nothing wrong with the suits."

"That is for me to decide."

Andrine chewed her lip, shaking her head. "The suits were all tested. If you ground the suits, we can't carry on our work here."

"Please, Andrine. You are making more conclusions. We will see. The truth will come out."

Lowering her voice, Andrine leaned forward over the desk. "Look, you can say no to this, but could I see your report before you send it off?"

"That is not the proper procedure."

"I know. But I need to know if I'm going to have to resign. This is my career here. I may even get prosecuted for this."

Enrico gazed into his whiskey and sighed, the Oberon case at the forefront of his mind. "Ah, we try to do our jobs, sì? And we make one mistake and everything is our fault. Andrine, I will let you see the report."

"Thank you, Enrico. I totally appreciate this. I won't let anyone else see it, I promise."

"Sì, sì. You are welcome."

"How long do you think it will take?"

"I need to complete it in no more than a few days."

"Why?"

"I must be on the mothership when it returns to Earth. The next one is not for two months. I cannot stay here that long. I cannot."

3) KIRSTEN FLAGSTAD SINGING "HO JO TO HO", FROM WAGNER'S *WALKURE*

Enrico sucked in through his teeth, peering through his magnifying glass at the lesion in Professor Terri Dawkins's spacesuit.

"Abrasion."

At Andrine's instruction, Lucy had brought him to the science labs. She hovered at his shoulder. "So, that little hole was all it took?"

"Sì. The edges of the hole are frayed. It is at the point where the helmet rubs on the neck material."

"Poor Terri."

An indignant snort came from behind them. Enrico turned to see an overweight, grey-haired woman scowling from the door of the labs. "Poor Terri. Yeah, right."

Lucy took a step forward. "Enrico, this is Professor Janice Brunthwaite, our remaining astrobiologist."

Janice strode into the room, slinging her holdall matter-of-factly under a bench. "Well done, Lucy. Astrobiologist, that was a long word. You were able to say it and stand up at the same time."

"That was unnecessarily rude, Janice. I do not have to put up with that from you."

"So, go somewhere else then. This is the science lab, not the chapel."

113

Enrico had been briefed about Janice. To his private amusement, "Ho jo To ho", The Ride of the Valkyries, started playing in his head. Kirsten Flagstad's Brunhilde provided the perfect backdrop to this encounter. "Madam, you are a very rude woman."

Janice laughed, mimicking Enrico's accent. "A very-ah rude-ah woman. You must-ah be our Health-ah and-ah Safety Officer."

"Madam, I have a job to do here."

"Yeah, well so do I. It's bad enough having to pick up the pieces of Terri's botched research, with Mother Teresa here trying to save my soul. Now I've got the Health and Safety mafia to put up with as well."

"Madam, your colleague has died. You have no respect? You should be ashamed."

"No, I'm not ashamed. I have the courage to be honest. I have no respect for Terri's work. She should not have been on this mission." Janice pointed a finger at the wall. "She should not have gone out there on her own. If she hadn't done that, she wouldn't be dead but, knowing Terri, I expect she wanted all the glory for anything she might find. And yes, it is poor Terri, I wish she hadn't died. But at least when I say it, I'm being honest, unlike Lucy here, who wants us all dead because she's terrified we're going to find something that upsets her stupid scriptures."

Lucy's eyes were ablaze. "How dare you. That's outrageous."

"It's the truth. You don't want us here."

"No, I don't. You shouldn't be here, wasting everyone's time. The ICRT only let you come on this mission so we could prove you wrong, once and for all. You will find nothing that can undermine the teachings of the scriptures."

"If it wasn't for the ICRT interfering, we would have found fossil organisms months ago."

Lucy turned abruptly to Enrico. "There are all these rocks this base is sat on, have they found a single fossil here? No."

"That's because we're on a basalt flow from an extinct volcano. You do not get fossils in volcanic rocks, you stupid..." Janice addressed Enrico. "The mission's sponsors are all ICRT people. They insisted the base was built here, ten kilometres from the nearest fluvial deposits. The whole mission has been deliberately sabotaged right off the bat."

Enrico held his hands up. "I do not care."

Janice opened her mouth to speak again but Enrico bellowed. "I do not care."

In the stunned silence that followed, Enrico counted the bars of the aria. He was not angry, not even remotely, merely playing a part and continuing to indulge his secret joke. The pace of the dramatic music in his head dictated when he could deliver his killer line. "I am grounding these spacesuits."

"What?" Janice gasped, horror on her face.

"They will return to Earth with me to check for design faults."

"No. That will take months. We've only got three months left before the NASA mission is closed."

"That is not my concern."

Lucy looked down, scarcely able to conceal her smile.

Janice's eyes narrowed, her shock giving way to fury. "You're one of them, aren't you? You're from the ICRT."

"I work for the Health and Safety Executive."

"Yeah, right. Andrine's going to hear about this."

Janice stormed from the room.

4) ENRICO CARUSO SINGING "LA DONNA E MOBILE", FROM VERDI'S *RIGOLETTO*

The man's badge labelled him as Mack Grayland, Engineer. He poured himself a coffee from the cafetière and glanced at Enrico. "Do you want one?"

Enrico nodded. "Sì. Grazie."

He had not expected the base's common room to be luxurious but was surprised at the lack of one particular facility. "There is a bar somewhere?"

"A bar? No, not here, buddy. Alcohol is against the rules."

Enrico looked quickly around. Nobody was close. "Do you have anything for me?"

"No. Sorry, there's no alcohol anywhere on the base." Mack smiled, and walked off to join his colleagues at the far end of the room.

Enrico found a spare easy chair and sank into it. The hot, strong coffee tasted good but he would have preferred one of Andrine's illicit miniatures. Her secret stash demonstrated once again her flagrant disregard for rules and procedures. It was a shame. Her casual attitude was going to cost her her job.

"Hi, Enrico. Can I join you?"

Looking up at Lucy, his spirits lifted. "Please." He ran his gaze over her long, slim legs as she folded herself into the easy chair opposite.

She smiled at him over the top of her coffee. "I'm sorry about Janice, earlier on."

"Ah, it is nothing. She is a very rude woman."

"She's furious at you. You've effectively stopped their silly mission."

Enrico shrugged. "That is not my concern. My job is to make sure there is no further trouble."

"Have you finished your report?"

He noticed an urgency about her question. "I have completed the first draft."

"Is Andrine, you know…" She drew a finger across her throat.

"My report goes to the Health and Safety Executive first."

"Okay, okay." She laughed and sipped her coffee.

He smiled at her. She was a beautiful woman. More beautiful than Katelyn. "Are you afraid of the *professores* finding fossils, like Janice said?"

"No. Because they won't find any."

"You are so certain?"

"Of course. The Divinity only created life on Earth."

"What about the fossils on Earth? Don't they show the Earth to be older than four thousand years B.C.? They are the remains of animals that are extinct."

"Oh, that old chestnut." She laughed. "A lot of these so-called fossils are really just rock formations. Things like the dinosaurs were all killed in the Flood. The world appears to be old because The Divinity created it like that. We know it isn't because the scriptures tell us the exact age of the Earth."

"The scriptures give you the truth and all these things that seem to prove it wrong can be explained somehow, sì?"

"Yes, absolutely."

"If there are fossils on Earth, why not fossils on Mars?"

"Because there was never any life on Mars."

"But you just said the fossils on Earth were not from life. So, finding fossils on Mars should be no problem."

A slight hesitancy crept into her voice. "Well, they won't be fossils, will they?"

"But why did The Divinity create the world like that? Why confuse us so?"

"I don't know. Who knows why The Divinity does things? Many things in life test us. We just have to have faith."

"And not ask questions?"

"Of course we can ask questions. But the answers can all be found in the scriptures, if you look for them and have eyes to see."

"And the answer is to have faith?"

"Yes."

"And not to ask questions."

Her eyes narrowed but he laughed and held his palms up. "I am sorry, Ms Fullick. I am teasing you. Of course the scriptures give us the truth we need. Of course. Many times in my life have I taken comfort in the scriptures."

She relaxed, her frown giving way to an almost childish relief. Beautiful, perhaps, but not the most sophisticated. Katelyn would run rings around a girl like this.

She took another sip from her coffee. "What's that thing in your ear, if you don't mind me asking?"

"I do not mind. It is my aural player. Music is my life. Like your scriptures give you truth, music gives me mine. It plays directly to my inner ear, as clear as if I were in a concert hall."

"That sounds pretty cool. Is it playing now?"

"Sì."

"What are you listening to, then?"

"Enrico Caruso singing 'La Donna e Mobile'. His voice is heaven." He realised further explanation was needed. "From Verdi's *Rigoletto*, opera?"

She wrinkled her nose. "Oh. Opera. I don't like that sort of thing."

He regarded her for a few seconds. The aria sang of the infidelity and fickle nature of women. Now he thought of it, she seemed a little scrawny for his taste. "I hope to be away from here tomorrow."

"Oh. Okay. I suppose there's no reason to hang around if you're done."

"Did you see Terri's body?"

"What? Oh, no. I'm quite glad, really. I don't like that sort of thing."

"Who found her?"

"Andrine. She went out looking for her."

"On her own?"

"Well, several search parties went out when Terri didn't come back. I don't know who was with Andrine."

"But the medical officer saw the body and certified the cause of death?"

"Well, yes. It's one and the same."

"What do you mean?"

"Andrine's the medical officer as well as the commander. We all have to double up a bit here. When I'm not leading the crew in prayer, I'm supply officer."

Enrico shook his head. He was slipping. Of course Andrine was the medical officer as well. He'd been briefed about that.

5) LEONTYNE PRICE SINGING "O PATRIA MIA",
FROM VERDI'S *AIDA*

"I can't really get out of it, can I? I've got to resign." Andrine lowered Enrico's report to the desk and leaned back in her chair.

"O Patria Mia", Leontyne Price's finest performance, rang out in Enrico's ears. It was the scene set on the banks of the River Nile. Enrico closed his eyes. He would have preferred to be on the banks of the River Nile himself. Anywhere, in fact, rather than here. "I am sorry, Andrine. I have to fill in my reports accurately."

Andrine was troubling. She seemed altogether far too calm about the impending end to what had been an illustrious career.

"Of course, Enrico. Thank you for letting me see this." She tapped a finger on the report. "Will you be returning to the mothership this morning?"

Enrico retrieved the report from the desk. "I have a few things I need to double check."

Andrine's eyes narrowed. "What sort of things?"

"Nothing important. Just a few figures. If you will excuse me."

6) LUCIANO PAVAROTTI SINGING "UNA FURTIVA LAGRIMA", FROM DONIZETTI'S *L'ELISIR D'AMORE*

It took Enrico a while to find what he was looking for under the electron microscope, but the evidence was clear. The higher magnification revealed the telltale mark of an incision by a sharp, metal blade on the fibres of the suit. Just enough to get a hole started. The abrasion was added afterwards, probably requiring a determined effort to fray the tough carbon fibres.

"*Merda.*"

He couldn't just ignore this. When the spacesuit was checked back on Earth, the cut would be noticed.

"*Merda.*"

It would be too easy for the suit just to have worn through, wouldn't it? No, of course, it had to be murder. Like he needed that right now.

He breathed deeply, concentrating on the voice of Pavarotti, the great tenor, and the lilting, gentle melancholy of the romanza. "Una Furtiva Lagrima", One Furtive Tear, sung by a fool who thought a love potion would win his sweetheart.

Love. Enrico sighed. Katelyn was leaving him. She had always said she would go. Until she finally went, he had never believed her.

Focussing his attention on the suit, he banished the chaos of his personal life to the back of his mind. There was a job to do and he was a professional. He had been briefed on the base's personnel. One or two oddballs but no real psychopaths. So then, who and why?

He clicked his tongue. "What did you find, Professor Terri Dawkins? What did you find?"

7) DAME KIRI TE KANAWA SINGING "PORGI, AMOR, QUALCHE RISTORO", FROM MOZART'S *LE NOZZE DI FIGARO*

"Janice, may I speak with you please?"

"Oh. Mister Health-ah and-ah Safety." Janice glowered up from her microscope. "You expect me to talk to you? You've grounded me."

"Please. Perhaps I can grant you some comfort, sì? I may be able to help you if you help me."

She shrugged. "What, then?"

Enrico took a seat at the bench beside her. They were alone in the laboratory but he spoke in hushed tones nevertheless. "I would like to know what Terri was working on before she died."

"The rock samples we managed to collect from the old river channels." She pointed to a box of slides beside the microscope. "We found some ancient cherts…"

"Cherts?"

"A type of sedimentary rock formed from silicon dioxide. They're exactly the same kind of rocks that a guy called Schopf found in Western Australia. Schopf's rocks were nearly three and a half billion years old and they were teeming with fossils of primitive cells."

"Three and a half billion years old. Ah, Janice, those are words that can get you into trouble."

"To hell with the ICRT. They don't scare me."

"They should do. They will be watching you."

"Ancient rocks can be dated using the radioactive decay of uranium two three eight. It has a half-life of four and a half billion years. The physics of radioactive decay are proven; the ICRT cannot argue with that."

"Janice, whether they are right or wrong, they are paying your wage. But no matter. Tell me, these chert samples you and Terri found?"

"Well, we slice them up real thin and look at them under the microscope to see if we can find any fossil bugs."

Enrico laughed. "And that's it? That's all you do?"

"That's it. And the ICRT is terrified because if we find something, it will make them look stupid."

"So, did Terri find any fossils?"

"Who knows? She was a selfish bitch, wouldn't let on." She snorted. "We all are. You ain't seen nothing as undignified as two competing scientists trying to get their work published before the other."

"So, she did not give you any clue?"

"Nope."

"But you collected the rocks together?"

For a moment, Janice seemed wrong-footed. "We have to go outside in groups of at least two." She smiled wryly. "For Health and Safety reasons, I guess."

Enrico thought for a moment. "Janice, take care. Sometimes the truth can be very dangerous."

8) MARIA CALLAS SINGING "VISSI D'ARTE", FROM PUCCINI'S *TOSCA*

"Andrine, may I walk with you?"

"Of course, Enrico. Did you finish your report?"

They made their way down a path between the pine trees, the deep sadness of soprano Maria Callas tugging at his heart: *Nell'ora del dolor, perchè, perchè, Signor, ah, perchè me ne rimuneri così?*—In the hour of sorrow, why, why, Lord, ah why reward me thus?

"I am sorry but I really need to see Terri's body."

"That's totally out of the question. Like I said, there is an autopsy report."

"The one written by you?"

A flicker of concern crossed Andrine's face. "As I am also medical officer here, I wrote the autopsy, yes."

"The spacesuit was cut, probably with a knife."

Andrine stopped, her face flustered. "That's impossible."

"It was cut. I suspect Terri's death was not due to equipment malfunction. She was murdered. You were the person who found her body, sì?"

"Yes."

"On your own?"

"I don't like where you're going with this."

"I'm going to the police unless you give me some very good answers. I would like to see Terri's body. Now, please."

Andrine turned away from him, nervously running her hand through her hair. "You can't…"

"I will have no choice but to tell the police."

"You can't." She turned back to him, tears in her eyes.

Enrico hated this. Why couldn't the stupid suit just have worn through? That would have made everything simple.

Andrine backed away from him. "Come to my office in ten minutes. Ten minutes, okay? I'll explain everything."

9) KATHLEEN BATTLE, ELISABETH SÖDERSTRÖM, AND FREDERICA VON STADE SINGING "THE FINAL TRIO", FROM RICHARD STRAUSS'S *DER ROSENKAVALIER*

Reluctantly, Enrico turned the Strauss down low and pressed an ear to Andrine's door. He could make out voices in the room beyond, at least two people. Were they going to try and jump him? Wearily, he brought the volume back up and knocked.

Andrine's voice came from beyond. "Come in."

He opened the door but did not enter. Andrine sat behind her desk, with Janice and a second woman sitting in front of it. Andrine beckoned to him hastily. "Come in, please."

Glancing to the left and right, he cautiously entered the room, closing the door behind him. The new woman was younger, maybe thirty, with short brown hair and large glasses. She chewed her nails anxiously.

"Please, Enrico, take a seat. This is a little embarrassing for all of us."

Enrico sat between the two women. "Why?"

"This is Terri."

"*Merda*." He buried his face in his hands. "*Merda*." With one hand still covering his face, he extended the other for Terri to shake. "Professor Terri Dawkins, how nice to meet you."

She shook hands feebly. "I know this must be a bit of a surprise."

"Madam, I am but pleased you are safe and well. I would just like to know why."

Andrine spoke. "I'm sorry, Enrico. Really I am. I'm not sure how to explain."

"Hell, I am." Janice rolled up her sleeves. "We need your help, Enrico. Terri found evidence of extinct life in those chert samples. Lots of life, and it's complex as well. Multi-cellular organisms. It's the ICRT's worst nightmare: incontrovertible evidence that life existed on Mars in abundance about three billion years ago."

Terri touched him on the arm. "We've kept it very quiet. Only Andrine, Janice, and I know about it because the ICRT will do anything they can to stop it getting out."

"They've bugged the labs, they've bugged my office. I go around with a detector and squash them all but every few days, more turn up." Andrine leaned closer, her voice a whisper. "We are afraid, Enrico. Really afraid. If this discovery gets back to Earth, it could seriously undermine the authority of the ICRT. This isn't about science or truth; this is about power."

Enrico looked up from his hands. "But why is Terri here? You said she was dead?"

"We faked her death. She's going in the casket onto the mothership, with the rock samples. Once she's on the ship, she can transmit the findings back to Earth. The ICRT won't be able to kill her once she's on the mothership. It would be too high profile."

"Why not transmit your findings from here?"

"Because all the transmissions get routed through a queuing system in the Communications Centre. The ICRT is monitoring

123

the queue. It's Lucy, she's doing it. She thinks I don't know. But they can't stop transmissions from the mothership."

Janice now touched Enrico's arm. "You could help us. We were worried Terri might not be able to get out of the casket once it was on the mothership. You could help her get out."

"*Merda.* This is crazy talk, crazy. You faked a professional rivalry to hide your fossils from Lucy? You faked Terri's death in order to smuggle her onto the mothership?"

"Yes." Janice grinned. "And of course, the accident is already big news. The spotlight's on us. You wait. When dead Terri jumps up to explain we found life and we had to do this because the ICRT was trying to gag us, the papers will go crazy. The story will be everywhere. It will be unstoppable. We'll bring the ICRT to its knees."

"Will you help us, Enrico? Please. I'm terrified of going in the casket. If I know you're there to get me out, it will be more bearable. I get quite claustrophobic."

"Please, do not ask me to do this."

"Enrico, please help us." Andrine sighed. "Didn't you tell me the truth will always come out? This is the truth, Enrico, the biggest truth of your life. We need you, Enrico. Will you help us?"

He sat up, the crescendo of voices playing in his ears bringing no comfort. If only he could help these three desperate, hopeful women. If only he could do the right thing. If only he could say no.

"Sì."

10) DMITRI HVOROSTOVSKY SINGING "THE DEATH OF RODRIGO", FROM VERDI'S *DON CARLO*

Enrico flumped down into the chair and shrugged across the desk at Alex. "It is finished. The warrant has been issued for the arrest of Andrine Hucknell and Janice Brunthwaite. They will be charged with the murder of Professor Terri Dawkins."

Alex leaned back in his seat, folding his arms behind his head. "You can lose the cod-Italian accent now, buddy."

"I'm sorry." Enrico's accent vanished. "I keep slipping back into it. Three months under cover and an accent sticks, you hear what I'm saying?" He placed a little box of microscope slides and a datastick of files on the desk. "This is Terri's research."

"You've done a good job, buddy."

"I feel bad, Alex, real bad. I let her die in the casket."

"Hey, come on, enough of the introspection. You gave her a nitrogen canister instead of an oxygen one, right? So she wouldn't even have known she was suffocating. She'd have just drifted off to a happy dream where she wins the Nobel Prize. Hell, you did her a favour."

That at least was true. The human body only knows it is asphyxiating from a build-up of carbon dioxide. Enrico shook his head. "They trusted me. Hell, they thought Lucy Fullick was one of our agents."

Alex chuckled. "She'd probably have made a better job of it than Mack Grayland. Deep cover? Deep schmover. Did he contact you at all while you were up there?"

"I spoke to him but he had nothing for me. He hadn't figured what was going on."

"The guy's heading for a desk job, you hear what I'm saying? If you hadn't gone up there, this might have got out." Alex gestured at the slides.

"You know what, Alex? I wish it had. You look at those slides, they're full of fossils. Mars must have been crawling with life three billion years ago. The scientists were right."

"Yeah, so? Who cares? What difference does it make? You want to destabilise society just because once upon a time, there were a few bugs on Mars? If this gets out, it will cause chaos. Civil rights lawyers will appeal against all the blasphemy law convictions. Every trouble-causer we've locked up for the last twenty years will be back out on the streets. We want people to be happy. The ICRT makes them happy. They don't have to think, they don't have to worry. They can watch the ball game, watch the talk shows, do a little shopping, no complications, and everything can keep running smoothly. Don't talk to me about bugs."

A few moments of silence passed. Alex leaned forward again. "Look, buddy, if it's any consolation, we've got some dirt on the prosecutor in the Oberon case. He's being very cooperative. You're in the clear."

Enrico stole a moment with his music, his precious, consoling opera. "Katelyn wants the house. She didn't pay a penny towards it. It's my damned house."

"We appreciate what you've done. Hell, I appreciate what you've done. I know this is a bad time for you."

The aria reached its climax. "The Death of Rodrigo", a man murdered for the incriminating, politically sensitive documents entrusted to him by a friend. "I've had it with killing people, Alex. I want my next assignment to be simple, okay? No complications."

Alex laughed, stretching back in his chair again. "Yeah, like when is anything simple, buddy? When is anything simple?"

The Last First Night

Charlotte Bond

Charlotte writes because she feels that otherwise her head might implode with all the imagined worlds within it. As well as "The Last First Night", Charlotte has had short stories published in both print and electronic format, spanning the genres of fantasy, science fiction, and horror. Charlotte lives in West Yorkshire with her husband and an extraordinarily fluffy cat.

127

The sun was setting in a magenta glow, colouring the full harvest moon a sickly hue, when the lord of the castle rode down into the tithe-village. The crowd gathered in the market place ceased its celebrations and parted to let him pass. Children shied away as he rode through them, and even full-grown men averted their eyes fearfully. A dog slunk towards the horse and bared its teeth at the rider. The lord replied with a snarl of his own, teeth just as sharp and vicious as the beast's, and the dog scampered away squeaking its fear.

The girl watched him ride up on his darkling steed, its eyes wide, nostrils flaring. The flicker of a smile on her beautiful face was quickly chased away by a blank expression.

She told herself: I will show no fear because I have none. She passed her poesy of white heather to her attendants and clasped her hands in front of her to stop them trembling. Her new husband had no such presence of mind and he shook like the last leaf in an autumn gale.

The lord regarded them with a cold stare, his long black hair tied behind his neck, mimicking his steed's twitching tail. He had fine sculpted cheekbones, full red lips perhaps a little too large for his face, and thick wiry eyebrows which formed one stern line over his countenance. The girl could not deny he was young and handsome.

As her husband shuffled backwards in fear, her father took a bold, protective step forward.

"I come to claim the right of *jus primae noctis* as your overlord," the lord stated. His voice was like a valley river, dangerous undercurrents roiling beneath the silken surface.

"Please, my lord," said her father, the quaver in his voice belying his firm expression. "We have a merchet for you instead, a bride-tax in place of our daughter." The father held up a bulging skin of coins but the lord knocked it away with a snarl.

"You cannot deny me my ancient heir-born right," the lord said in a low, menacing voice. "All brides married under a full harvest moon are mine for one night before they belong to their husband."

"But it's the most auspicious night upon which to be married," piped up her stout mother, tears flowing down her once rosy cheeks. "It ensures long life, happiness, and fertility."

"Such boons do not come without a price to be paid—to me," the lord growled impatiently. He regarded the girl. "You will come with me now," he commanded.

The girl embraced her weeping mother, kissed her fearful husband, and bowed to her reluctant father. He embraced her fiercely.

"Pay attention, girl," he muttered quickly into her ear. "That simple silver chain around your neck belonged to your grandmother. She wore it on her wedding night, too. It is a talisman, so take heart from it." The girl inclined her head slightly to show she understood and then climbed up on the horse behind her lord. Her white dress cascaded like a waterfall over the mount's dark hind. She had never ridden anything larger than the water-ponies and it seemed a long way down to the hard earth. Her nerves fluttered as the beast trotted homewards and she clung tightly to the lord, burying her face in his hair. As her slender fingers gripped his open doublet for balance, she was surprised to realise how much thick, wiry hair covered his chest.

The girl had seen the castle from a distance but never appreciated its size and grandeur until she stood within its courtyard. The lord helped her down from his steed and led her through the rooms one by one. She marvelled at their splendour, her breath coming in delighted gasps. Her hovel-home was forgotten as she wandered and wondered. She was entranced as she floated through more rooms than she could count.

"This room will be yours for the night," the lord said, opening the final closed door. They walked into a room hung with rich tapestries and dominated by a canopied mahogany bed. "You will find suitable attire for the feast in here," he said, opening a chest filled with shimmering satins and damasks. The girl bowed slightly to show she knew her duty and stood aside to let him leave. As the lord passed, he paused and tilted her downcast face towards him. This close she could see his eyes were the verdant green of the forest, flecked with a glittering gold; she could make out every fine hair of his immaculately groomed beard.

"You are not afraid," he commented. She smiled demurely.

"I could be, if it would please you, my lord," she replied. As he drew breath to reply, his lips formed a silent snarl of disgust as he saw the chain about her neck. He stepped away from her.

"What would please me," he said, "would be for you to remove such pauper's trinkets and wear the gold and jewels which you will find on the boudoir." He smiled gallantly, wickedly. "No lady of mine shall wear anything but the finest."

The girl bowed again to show her obedience, but smiled to herself; she had seen through his ruse. She removed the necklace and laid it on the table next to her. The lord smiled once with satisfaction, then once again with greed and she saw how long and knife-sharp his incisors were.

~

The feast was sumptuous, the air heady with wine fumes and spices. Meat from every animal in the realm was offered the lord's guests, who brawled over it like dogs. The girl noticed that their teeth were just as sharp as their lord's.

The tables groaned with extravagant dishes of barely-cooked game, glistening with bloody juices. The girl swallowed a mouthful of warm wine to slake her thirst and then reached out to take a slice of venison. In a flash, her lord's hand had encompassed her slender wrist and drawn it back.

"No lady of mine will have to suffer such base victuals," he said with a soft smile which didn't quite reach his eyes. "I have something sweeter for my sweetheart." He beckoned and a servant stepped between the quarrelling, snapping guests. He carried a golden platter laid out with plump fruits, some native, some exotic, all tempting. The lord picked out a Physalis, crushing its paper casing between his palms, then offering the exposed fruit to her lips. The girl shivered involuntarily, remembering the tales of Persephone and her pomegranates, but she closed her eyes and bit into the fruit to please the lord. Please him it did, and he watched her sample another, his eyes heavy with wine and desire before dismissing her from the table. The girl bowed in submission and retired to her room, where she found an identical platter of fruit next to her bed. She went to the table and picked up her grandmother's chain, clutching it close for courage. Then she picked up the small fruit knife lying on the platter and set to work.

When the lord flung open her door later that night, nigh on the witching hour, the girl was reclining and ready on the bed. She was dressed in a silk bridal shift and a torque of gold encircled her white throat. The platter lay at her feet, each piece of fruit meticulously sliced and cored. She gestured towards it as the lord approached hungrily.

"Something sweet for my lord?" she asked demurely. She could hear the feast continuing in the hall below, the cries of the revellers now raised to drunken shrieks and bestial howls. In five strides her lord crossed the room and swept the platter off the bed, scattering fruit everywhere.

"I have a better appetite for meat," he said gruffly. She saw the shimmer of saliva on his lips, the darkness that had blossomed beneath his heavy brows; she saw that his eyes— now completely golden—stared out of that darkness like those of a starved predator. She could smell the rosemary oil in his hair, mingled with something deeper, like the forest after the rain. And she could hear the growl that started in his throat then bristled across his whole body, just before he leapt at her.

She was ready for him. As his face came so close that the longest hairs of his beard stroked her cheek, his movements ceased. The gold flickered in his eyes and then was gone, leaving green eyes flecked with surprise. The lord in his castle looked down to see what separated him from his quarry and he saw the ivory handle of the fruit knife protruding from his chest.

The girl realised she had been holding her breath and she let it out slowly as she withdrew the dagger. "I have bowed to you three times today," she said softly. "Now you will bow before me."

The lord looked in horror and no small measure of surprise at the simple silver chain wrapped around the blade. The weapon glinted cruelly in the candlelight, even beneath its coat of blood. He looked beseechingly at his stolen bride and saw a reflection of his own cold smile. Then death stole all life from his eyes and he fell forward at the girl's feet.

Realising her breath was coming in ragged, relieved gasps, the girl paused to steady her nerves. Then she hauled the body out the door, heaved it onto the balustrade, and pushed it over so that, even in death, the lord of the castle could participate in his feast. Growls, bellows, and wails rose from the hall below, almost—but not quite—covering the sound of claws ripping into flesh. The girl peeked over the edge and it was as if she looked into the pit of Hell itself. The castle revellers fought each other for the final scraps of meat, furry muzzles snapping and snarling fiercely.

Closing her door on the scene below, the girl picked up one of the scattered pieces of fruit and then curled up on the bed. She peeled the pomegranate with care, picking out and eating the seeds one by one, until the first rays of dawn crept up the walls.

The Oath

Murphy Edwards

Edwards's writing has appeared in over fifty professional magazines and journals including Dimensions Magazine, The East Side Edition, Black October, MidAtlantic Monthly, Modern Drummer, The Nor'Easter, Walking Bones, Escaping Elsewhere, Trail of Indiscretion, Hardboiled Magazine, Barbaric Yawp, Samsara, The Magazine of Suffering, Horizons, and Dead Bait, the upcoming anthology by Severed Press. His short story "Hideyholes" was chosen to be among the best in science fiction, fantasy, and horror for the Leucrota Press Anthology, Abaculus II. Edwards's work to date includes excursions into horror, hard-boiled thrillers, crime mysteries, westerns, and contemporary fiction. He currently resides in Indiana.

Bud Jenkins called the meeting to order and the hay loft fell quiet. A bottle was passed around; it was a tradition. A pact had made the loft a necessity, and everyone involved had to take the oath. An oath of confidence. An oath of silence.

"Folks, we got some serious thinking to do. That last one filled up the only spot left in my back pasture. I've flat run out of room. What about you, Fred?"

Fred Strump finished his turn at the bottle and passed it on. He'd taken double pulls on the bourbon at every meeting since they found his wife and son cut up and stuffed in one of his out buildings like bundles of worm-rich trash. "I'm not sure the hogs can get rid of it fast enough. The one last week took a couple days. Myrtle sniffed out a stray bone and carried it around for a week straight. Just lucky I found it near her dog house and buried it under the corn crib." Fred rubbed his hands together and pulled at the joints in his fingers. His empty eyes held a vicious look that reflected the pain he was feeling. "Whatever we do with it is too good for it, in my book. I suppose we could sink it in my pond. Ain't done that for a while. If we weight it down good and proper, the catfish should pick it clean soon enough."

Jenkins waited for additional input from the others. None came. "That'll fix this one, but if we're going to continue we had best come up with a long-term solution.

Tina Sage waved off her turn at the bottle and adjusted her seat on a hay bale. "I really didn't think it would last this long. I figured once we thinned the herd a bit, and word got out, things would quiet down and get back to normal."

"Not likely," said Jenkins. "Seems to be no end to it. If anything, we got more now than we did a year ago. Let's face it, friends, the bodies are starting to stack up!"

~

Three years earlier, Bud Jenkins had brought in the best corn crop of his life. His new barn was paid for, and he managed to replace his aging truck with a newer model. For the first time in a decade, he had a positive balance in his checking account. The savings bank emergency fund was built back up and he even managed to replace the mismatched living room furniture. Life was good on the Jenkins Cattle Farm.

It was late August and Jenkins had been at a farm machinery show checking prices on a new tractor. He took the luxury of staying in a hotel over night to avoid a long drive home with little sleep. What he found when he returned changed his life forever.

The Sunday paper was still stuffed in the tube next to the unemptied mailbox. At the end of the lane, his daughter's car sat at an odd angle in the garage. The door was open and the interior light burned dimly. Small droplets of red were spattered on the seat and door panel. The garage floor was a crimson mess.

Jenkins found his daughter sprawled out on the back porch with a pitch fork in her back. The blood trail revealed a powerful struggle, one she had lost. He called 911. Forty-five minutes later, a deputy pulled into the driveway. Jenkins held his bleeding wife in his arms, rocking her like an infant. He had carried her out of the barn where he found her—unconscious and bleeding— slumped over a stack of salt blocks and seed corn.

At Venters County Hospital, Jenkins paced nervously, waiting for some word on his wife. The ER was a thirty minute ambulance ride from the farm, a ride that had allowed his wife to bleed out. She had coded twice during the trip, brought back by an alert EMT and a defibrillator. At 4:18 p.m., eight hours after discovering his family, a surgeon broke the news to

Jenkins. She was gone. In eight hours he had lost the family he had worked for thirty-five years to keep. All he had left was the farm.

The next morning, the deputy appeared on Jenkins's front porch before sunrise. The front door was still ajar, so he let himself in. Bud Jenkins remained in the kitchen chair where he'd been all night. The deputy listened to Jenkins's version of the events while nodding and taking notes in a small black notebook.

"Any idea at all who would do this to me and my family?"

"Meth heads," said the deputy, continuing to scribble. "They cruise the rural roads looking for ammonia."

"Ammonia?"

"Yep, ammonia. Well, more precisely, anhydrous ammonia."

"What the hell for?"

The deputy flipped to a new page. "They use it in the cooking process. You know, to make the drug. When they can't find that, they'll pretty much take whatever isn't nailed down or locked up."

Jenkins stared into a cold cup of coffee and shook his head. "You mean to tell me these thugs are murdering people over farm supplies?"

"That's the long and short of it."

"In the meantime, we just sit back and let them take over?"

The deputy slid the notebook back in his shirt pocket and buttoned it. "We'll take them to jail if we catch them, but it's hard—too much territory to cover and too few lawmen."

"I don't find that reassuring," Jenkins mumbled into his clenched fists.

"Mr. Jenkins, I'm truly sorry for your loss. I wish I could do something to make it right. I'd be the first to even the score if I could. Until we get some help out here, we rely on residents to keep an eye out and report anything suspicious. Not much else we can do."

Jenkins waited for the deputy to disappear down the driveway, then he picked up the phone. The following Monday, the first meeting was held in the loft. Along with Jenkins, Fred

Strump and five other neighbours agreed something drastic needed to be done. Soon. Everyone took the oath.

~

After considerable discussion, Harv Kettler, the neighbourhood gear head, volunteered to try and come up with a more permanent solution to their mounting disposal problems. He worked feverishly in the makeshift shop at the barn. The sound of heavy hammers striking sheet steel and rusted iron echoed off the shop walls, while blue-white welding arcs flashed through gaps in the burlap sacks hung loosely over the dust-covered windows. After two weeks of pounding, hacking, grinding, and patching, Harv summoned everyone to the shop for the unveiling.

Kettler waited for everyone to get settled, then closed the barn door and slid an iron bar through the latch. In the centre of the barn floor was a large object draped in mouldy canvas tarps.

"Folks, I've given our dilemma a considerable amount of thought. Took several days to get all the bugs out, but I think I've got a perfect solution to our problem."

Marvin Hester lifted his cap and rubbed his bald head with a calloused hand. "Come on, Harv! Pull the sheet off this damned thing and let's get this show on the road! I still got feedin' and milkin' to do!"

"Soon enough. Just wanted to let you know where I'm coming from on this. If anyone isn't full-on in favour, we walk straight back out that door and forget everything. Clear?"

The barn was silent.

"Go ahead," said Jenkins.

Kettler grabbed a dusty corner of the tarp, holding it out like a magician in the midst of some awesome slight of hand. "I present to you—The Chunkster!"

The tarp floated to the ground and revealed a hulking mish-mash of used and discarded farm equipment and household appliances. Heavy welds and stainless bolts held cutting disks and plough blades at odd and dangerous angles. A narrowing chute ran at a steep downward angle through the blades and into a dark opening in the machine.

Jenkins spit into a loose pile of straw and looked down the chute. "What exactly does this thing *do*, Harv?"

"It gets rid of our problems. What else?"

Before anyone could ask how, Kettler reached into the closest stall, snatched up a piglet, and flipped a toggle switch on the side of the machine. The piglet kicked and squealed, fighting the grip Kettler had on its neck.

When the machine had powered up completely, he slid the squealing animal onto the chute and gave it a shove. Everyone watched as the blades and cutters quartered the piglet like an apple. The quarters disappeared down the opening and into the machine.

Kettler moved to the back of the machine and opened a large metal door. A lump of pulp the size of a piglet dropped to the barn floor. "There you have it, friends."

"That's all well and good," Marvin Hester said, still rubbing his head. "But we still got that lump of stuff left to get rid of."

Kettler grinned. "That's the beauty of it. Remember how high our heating bills got last year? Most of us had to take out loans just to keep our houses heated."

"Don't need you to remind me of that. I'm still paying that one off. How has that got a damned thing to do with this, though?"

Kettler walked to the far end of the barn and lifted another tarp. "It's got *this* to do with it."

Bud Jenkins began to grin. "Harv, ain't that one of them new wood stoves that burns pellets and wood pulp?"

"Sure is. Heats an average home for about eight cents a day plus material costs. Cool to the touch, but gets hotter than double hell on the inside. Burns any kind of wood. Once the stuff from The Chunkster dries out, it'll burn that too."

Tina Sage jumped off her perch on the corral and dusted off her ass with a slap. "Kettler, you are a genius."

"Pretty much."

~

138

In less than a month, every farmer in the neighbourhood had installed a new wood stove. The salesman from the stove company was happier than a Triple-K lottery winner.

"Folks around here must be expecting a harsh winter," he said, while checking the fittings on Bud Jenkins's stove.

"It tends to get a little harsh in this part of the country," Jenkins smirked. "Mostly in the last five or six years."

"Better safe than sorry," said the salesman, giving the ducting a final check.

"You got that right."

A week after the last stove was installed, Marvin Hester came tearing into Jenkins's barnyard throwing gravel and rocks in a wide arc above his truck. Jenkins put down the bucket of feed he was carrying and waited for Hester to get out.

"Bud, I need help! Quick!"

"What's the problem?"

"Walked up on two of them at the back of my pasture. Had the tool box on my harvester broken open and were making off with most of the tools inside. I had to run them down with the truck."

"Where are they now?"

Hester lifted a sheet of blue plastic in the bed of his truck. Two bloodied males lay motionless underneath, their eyes frozen wide with fear.

"Shit, Hester! What the hell are you bringing them here for? In broad daylight?! We got a method for dealing with this now! Remember?"

"It goes a little deeper than that. They didn't die right off. One of them told me he knew what we were doing out here. Said he'd filed a report with the authorities already."

"That's bullshit! He was bluffing to get you to let him go." Jenkins looked in the truck at the lifeless bodies. "Don't guess he'll have to worry about that now."

"I'm telling you he knew something. He named Harv by his full name. He said he knew who 'The Builder' was and what we were using for fuel out here."

"Impossible! How could he know all that? We've had an oath for over five years. Why would anyone break it now?"

Marvin Hester paced the barnyard and stared at his weathered boots. A puddle of blood pooled under his truck bed. "This don't look good, Bud. What if we get caught? What if they *did* report us?"

"Relax. Nobody is going to get caught." Jenkins looked in Hester's truck bed again, poking at a lifeless, tattooed arm with a twig. "Besides, if *you* were a cop, and one of these worthless shitheels came crawling into the station to report a crime, would *you* take them seriously?"

"I suppose not. Still...I don't like taking chances. Maybe we should drive on into town and come out with it. You know? I mean the sheriff already said most of these jokers have a rap sheet the size of a phone book. They'd likely go easy on us. May even give us a reward."

"Hester, we've been in this community for over thirty years. Before that, our parents owned this land. Why would the cops suspect us of butchering anything other than a beef cow or buck deer? As far as a reward goes, I wouldn't count on that. You saw what they did to the bastard that took my Ruthie. He's due out on parole next year for good behaviour. Good behaviour! Ain't that rich?!"

"But still—" Hester said.

"Still my ass! They'd put us away forever, then add ten years for good measure!"

Hester fell quiet. The blood dripped from his truck bed like a ticking clock.

"Come on. Let's get these two over to Harv's and be done with it. With any luck they'll be dry enough for the stove by the weekend."

~

Harv Kettler's one weakness was the Wednesday auctions at Pine Hill Farm Market. He rarely bought anything more than a hammer or an odd stick of furniture, but he liked the chance to catch up on the local gossip. Bud and Marvin got to Harv's at around noon—too early for him to be back from the auction. Bud decided not to wait for him before processing the thugs in

Hester's truck. He lowered the tailgate and rolled back the blue plastic.

Hester paced in wide circles around the truck while staring into his bloodstained palms. Sweat streamed down his cheeks and pooled on his chin. "I'm telling you, Bud, this just doesn't feel right."

"It's never bothered you before."

Hester ground his palms together. "To tell you the truth, I never..."

"Do you remember Fred? That look on his face when he collapsed in the court room? How that rat-faced judge added insult to injury by powder-puffing the sentence he gave the worm that took his family? A mental facility instead of giving him what he deserved? You call that justice? Hell, that punk should be on death row right now!"

"We should call the deputy—let him deal with it. I can tell him it was self-defence—they threatened me—pulled a weapon."

"And how do you propose explaining the bodies being moved, sitting in a truck bed at Kettler's place, a good five miles from where it happened?"

Hester fidgeted nervously with his cell phone.

"You got no weapon, no witnesses, no sign of a struggle, not even a scuff or a bruise. It'll never wash. Killing two guys for simple theft and trespassing—that's still manslaughter—maybe even first degree murder. Best think it through."

"Couldn't we just—"

"No! We do what we gotta do. Remember the oath."

Hester's fingers poked anxiously at the keypad. Beads of salty sweat hung from his upper lip. He tried to dial 911 three times. Each time he backed out and disconnected.

On the fourth attempt, Bud chucked the cell phone in The Chunkster and slapped Hester hard across the face. He waited for Hester to compose himself, then handed him a hip flask full of scotch. "Drink that and let's get this over with."

The first one loaded into the chute easily. A five-year meth habit had left little more than leathery skin stretched over rotting bones.

141

Hester struggled with the second thief, working up a lively sweat in the process. He began to sob and swear. "Come on, Bud. Give me a hand will you? I think this one is stuck."

Bud Jenkins put a heavy shoulder into Hester's back and shoved hard. The Chunkster bogged down slightly, dimming the lights in the barn before roaring back to full power. At the opposite end of The Chunkster, three neat little pulp lumps rolled out and dropped to the barn floor.

Hester's only known relative was in the East Conrad Nursing Home. The onset of Alzheimer's had left his Uncle Dave totally without memory of Hester, the farm, or the mountain of debt Hester had created trying to keep things afloat. After a brief investigation and a dozen interviews, the authorities were convinced Marvin Hester had disappeared of his own accord to avoid foreclosure and bankruptcy.

~

February. The dead of winter. Bud Jenkins fought through the snow-drifted back roads and pulled into the rutted gravel parking lot at Franklin Seed and Supply. The warehouse was cold and isolated, but Franklin Nealy always had a fresh pot of coffee and the latest gossip. Jenkins needed a little of both.

Fred Strump and the deputy sat in the warmth of the store, chairs tilted back, each holding a steaming mug in their hands. "Pull up a chair, Bud. Coffee just perked and Franklin just stoked the fire."

Jenkins eyed the deputy's boot heels resting on the hearth of Franklin Nealy's wood stove. "Don't mind if I do. What's the latest?"

Fred Strump sipped his coffee, letting the steam crawl up his nose and loosen his sinuses. "Deputy was just tellin' us how much crime has dropped lately."

Jenkins added sugar to his coffee and stirred it with a broken plastic fork from Nealy's workbench. "That so?"

"Yep. I haven't had a single complaint in the last two months."

Jenkins blew on the rim of his mug, sending puffs of steam over the deputy's shoulder. "Huh. How do you explain that? The weather?"

The deputy shifted in his chair, making the back legs wobble and crack, and continued to warm his feet on the stove. "I figure the meth heads have picked the area clean, you know? Just headed for greener pastures…so to speak."

Jenkins stopped blowing. "And now they're terrorizing some other community, stealing anything they please and killing anyone who gets in the way?"

Fred Strump slid his index finger over his pursed lips, signalling Jenkins to hush.

The deputy moved closer to the stove. "Not saying it's right, but sometimes these things have a way of working out on their own."

Jenkins took a long pull off his coffee. "Seems more like shifting the problem instead of fixing it."

"Don't get me wrong," the deputy continued. "I feel sorry for anyone else who has to deal with these creeps, but hey, better them than us, right? Besides, if I did what I'd like to do with these guys, I'd lose my badge."

Bud Jenkins was amused by the deputy's "no news is good news" attitude. *If only he weren't so incredibly naive,* Jenkins thought, *perhaps we could have been friends.*

~

Jenkins sat at his kitchen table next to a cold plate of bacon and eggs and read the front page of the Rural Rambler for the fifth time. The headline burned into his brain.

LOCAL FARMER AGREES TO SELL TO LAND DEVELOPER

How could Kettler do it? He'd been a farmer longer than any of them and in less than a week, he'd be flying to Chicago to sign a six-figure contract. The meth heads were dealt with. The crop futures were steady. No one was looking for Marvin any more. The recent hail damage had been covered by crop insurance. Now, instead of the dopers and thieves, they would have to cope with traffic, crowds, noise, and an endless stream of strangers who thought every square inch of the country was created for their own personal pleasure.

Jenkins broke out a fresh bottle of bourbon. He would call an emergency meeting in the loft first thing in the morning. By tradition, a vote was required. He had little doubt of the outcome. It was a matter of survival.

The Ransom

Monique Frangi

Monique Frangi is a writer and English teacher living in Sydney, Australia. She is inclined towards stories that explore the dark side of human nature and promise something unexpected.

The silence of the house was broken by an urgent staccato knocking on the front door. Gaynor Wheeler, a middle-aged woman with her hair pulled back into an elegant chignon, pearls, and a tight-lipped mouth painted red, emerged from the Laura Ashley-inspired lounge to open the front door.

Detective Inspector Grahame stood on the doorstep with Senior Sergeant Hollister waiting beside him.

"Detectives, come in. Has there been any word?" Gaynor stood back and allowed the policemen to enter the house. She followed them through to the lounge.

"We were going to ask you that, Mrs. Wheeler." DI Grahame smiled.

Gaynor motioned to the men to sit. "Nothing," she advised them, her taut, red lips grim. "But you know that. Your people have been monitoring both my phone and mail since I notified you."

DI Grahame sat on the couch, whilst Hollister idled by the mantelpiece. "Your husband has been missing now for a week. It's unusual for the kidnappers not to have made some form of contact by now if money was the object." He paused and looked pointedly at the woman sitting upright opposite him.

Once again, her lips stretched grimly. "I understand. There is some concern then…" She swallowed thickly. "There is some concern for his well-being, then? I mean, for his life."

Her visitor nodded. "Indeed, I should say there is." He looked over at Hollister who shuffled uncomfortably and moved to inspect the contents of a bookcase. Gaynor followed the detective's gaze. There was a short pause: of expectation on her part, of discomfort on theirs.

She leaned forward. "Detective Grahame, I understand the seriousness of this situation. I am absolutely frantic about finding my husband. If there is something that you need to ask me, please do not hesitate."

"I want to ask you again about the state of your marriage." He half raised a work-weary hand of pre-emptive understanding. "I know how invasive it is to have strangers ask personal questions, but any information will help—if you're totally candid."

She sat back and eyed the detective in confusion. "You think that he left? That he abandoned me? Without a word?" Her tone was not accusing; rather, she seemed herself to have just realised the possibility.

Hollister came and joined his superior on the couch. "We must consider all the options. Your husband retired recently. It is not uncommon for men who have retired to be a bit, shall we say, toey, a bit restless."

Gaynor looked from one man to the other, her face a window of a mind working through an unexpected scenario.

"There is no easy way to bring this up," Detective Grahame ventured apologetically. "But we have found evidence among your husband's mobile phone records of a number that he was calling almost on a daily basis."

"A number?" Her eyes watched the men guardedly, protecting herself against the future direction of the conversation.

"It appears from our enquiries that your husband was regularly visiting a woman in Bella Vista."

Both men waited in respectful appreciation for the woman's shock.

"I see," she said quietly, her eyes steely in their understanding. "And you know this how?"

"We have spoken to this woman. Apparently you know her. From a previous time." The detective intoned it as a question.

"From a previous time? You mean, from a previous affair?"

The detective nodded. Gaynor Wheeler pursed her lips and stood up stiffly out of the armchair. "Gentlemen, at this point, I feel I need to pour myself a drink. Do you mind?"

"Please, go right ahead." The men listened to her as she moved in the adjoining kitchen. Ice clinked into a glass and there followed a splash of liquid. There was a moment of silence in which both men envisaged a beleaguered woman downing a quick swig of scotch.

She returned to the armchair, nursing the drink on her lap, her posture as correct as before. "I see," she murmured again. "Bella Vista," she noted dryly. "Well, yes, I do believe I recall that one."

Hollister glanced discreetly at DI Grahame. "You mean he's had more than one affair?"

"Yes, at least another three that I know of."

"How did you find out about them?" DI Grahame asked.

Gaynor shrugged. "The box of Viagra in his bathroom cupboard was the giveaway. I knew it wasn't on my account. But there are always signs. A woman knows."

"May I ask how you responded to this?"

A bitter smile. "I asked him to stop. On the last occasion, I told him if he did it again I would leave him."

"Why did you not tell us about this earlier?" DI Grahame asked pointedly.

"What's the point? He's been kidnapped. Or so I thought."

From his pocket, DI Grahame's mobile phone rang shrilly. He reached into his pocket, apologising and excusing himself from the room.

Hollister regarded the woman sympathetically. "It must've hurt to have discovered the other women. How did you manage to move on?"

Gaynor Wheeler looked back at him shrewdly. "I'm a fifty-six-year-old woman. I do not work. I have lived in this house with the same man for thirty-two years. I have three grown children. There is no question about what to do. One makes the choices necessary to keep one's life on track."

DI Grahame re-entered the room. He stood beside the couch staring at his phone, lost in thought.

"Sir?" Hollister enquired.

His superior looked at the woman sitting stiff and composed in the armchair. "Mrs. Wheeler, when did your husband disappear?"

Gaynor looked at the detective as if he were a stranger and not a regular visitor to the house over the past seven days.

"Sir?" Hollister detected a change in his partner's demeanour.

"Mr. Wheeler's body has been found." DI Grahame knew there was only ever one chance to view a first reaction. "You rang us regarding his disappearance last Thursday. Your husband has been dead since at least last Tuesday."

Gaynor placed her drink decisively on the coffee table. "Detective, are you suggesting that I murdered my husband? Because I should like to ring my lawyer now."

The detective shook his head in disbelief. "Actually, no, I'm not suggesting you murdered your husband. But you see, there is one troubling little piece of communication that was found with the body. And, honestly, I don't quite know where that leaves us—with you, I mean."

"Well, Detective, how about you share that information with me and perhaps I can help." The air in the room had turned tense.

"A note was found with the body, which incidentally had all his identification intact. The note was addressed to you."

Gaynor's eyebrows rose. "Indeed? And what did it say?"

"Specifically, 'Mrs. Wheeler, the deadline for the ransom is passed. You're an evil bitch. Here's your husband back.'"

"How terrible. That must be one letter that got lost in the post. Perhaps it will turn up later."

Gaynor Wheeler's red-lipped smile grew wide.

A Simple Smile

Christopher Roy Denton

Chris Denton is a middle-aged working class Yorkshire bloke who enjoys all forms of writing, from crime to science fiction, and from poetry to novels. He follows in the footprints of giants, since he lives in Thornton village where the four famous Brontë siblings were born. Chris is currently working on a novel set in modern-day Thornton with the working title *Masala*. The most significant people in Chris's life are his three sons: Daniel, Oliver, and Edward. He prays they will outshine him in every aspect of their lives.

James Flanagan twisted the rear view mirror to check his disguise one last time. He adjusted the cheap tie, ensuring it didn't look too neat. His short, red hair looked overdue for a haircut…perfect. Appearance mattered in his line of work. When he met the witness protection team, he wanted them to see a fellow cop rather than a hired killer. He even packed a Glock 21, knowing LAPD officers favoured this handgun in spite of criticism it suffered from explosive malfunctions.

The detective driving him to the safe house frowned and then twisted the mirror back into position. Outside the air-conditioned comfort of their unmarked police car, the midsummer sun sucked the life out of the desert. A hot, dry wind blew dust across the freeway, turning the metal sails of a dozen gigantic windmills. Because it was Sunday, they hadn't seen much traffic since leaving LA. A green sign came in sight, State Highway 111. They turned off the interstate toward Palm Springs.

James took a manila envelope from his jacket pocket and emptied the contents onto his lap. He'd seen these photographs before but it wouldn't hurt to take one last look at the face of his intended target. He turned to the sergeant. "Maloney, when we get there, just wait in the car."

The skinny officer nodded and attempted a grin. "Yessir!"

Something about Maloney disturbed him, but he couldn't quite put his finger on it. Maybe the problem lay in the way the man had been so easily bought. James had only brought the corrupt policeman this far because a familiar face would put the protection team at ease, bolstering James's credibility. He always eliminated all the witnesses following a hit. Killing the sergeant would be a genuine pleasure.

In high school, James had been dubbed "Dim Jim". He wasn't dim, but he looked it. The other students ridiculed him because he suffered from a mild but chronic form of facial muscular dystrophy. His appearance belied the cunning mind behind this deceptive mask. Many people had underestimated his intelligence and skill, with fatal consequences. He was not the first professional to take a crack at this particular mark. When other assassins failed, James was the man they called.

James studied the photographs, some detailed notes, and a layout diagram of the house. He ran through his plan, and then turned to Maloney. "So, the officer in charge is Sergeant Hoffman?"

His informant nodded. "He's the fat, bald guy in a light-grey suit. He'll probably be wearing Ray-Bans."

They passed through the outer limits of town and found the sidewalks deserted in the midday heat. Avoiding the centre of Palm Springs, they drove to the safe house: a two-story, pueblo-style home on a suburban street, surrounded by tall palm trees and a well-irrigated, bright green lawn.

As they pulled into the driveway, James saw no evidence of life in the neighbourhood. Not one dog barked or bird perched on a roof top...not even a vulture. The house appeared deserted. Ten seconds later, the Venetian blinds at one of the smaller windows briefly parted. He assumed at least one gun was now aimed at the car.

The front door of the yellow, adobe dwelling opened just wide enough to allow a fat, balding man wearing a grey suit to step cautiously out onto the porch. A second, much slimmer man stood close behind, but remained inside, half-hidden behind the door frame.

James climbed out of the vehicle, swearing as the blast of scorched air hit his face. Shielding his eyes from the glare of the sun, he waited for Hoffman to approach.

The fat man glanced through the open car window at the driver. Though the light of recognition shone in his eyes as he regarded Maloney, he still eyed James suspiciously.

The man toyed with a pair of sunglasses in his left hand. "Who're you? We were expecting Adams."

"I'm Stevenson. Adams couldn't make it."

The man frowned. "This is kinda irregular."

This was the point where James's particular skill came into use. He looked the sergeant straight in the eye and offered him the most genuine-appearing smile possible. James understood all too well the value of a simple smile.

"Hoffman?" asked James, offering his right hand.

The witness protection officer stared at James's hand for a few seconds, and then looked him in the face. He couldn't help but return the infectious smile and clasped James's hand.

James enjoyed exploiting his victim's instinctive compulsion to return a smile and handshake. He grasped the man's hand in a vice-like grip, feeling the warm, sweaty flesh squash against his own clammy skin. A confused look entered the man's eyes, and they flicked down toward their joined hands.

A tiny drop of bright-red blood ran down James's wrist. The man's eyes locked with James's as life drained out of them. James had hidden three tiny, pushpin-shaped applicators in his right palm. He had designed these lethal devices himself. Each pin could be employed up to five times. Each use injected enough venom to incapacitate an average man. The shock generated by three doses would kill anyone almost instantly. The man's knees buckled as he dropped and his sunglasses fell to the ground.

"Oh my God," shouted James. "He's having a heart attack."

The other officer rushed from the house, eyes wide. He hadn't seen any sign of violence, only a friendly exchange and handshake.

James's eyes oozed sympathy and compassion for the fallen man. He crouched beside the corpse, loosening its shirt and pretending to check for a pulse. The dead man's slim, blond-haired colleague looked on, fear for his friend painted in his eyes.

"His pulse is weak," lied James, "but I think he'll make it."

The officer knelt down beside his comrade.

James turned to him. "Want me to radio a paramedic?"

The policeman nodded, not removing his gaze from his friend.

154

James stood and patted him on the back before shifting his hand a few inches higher so his right palm slapped the man on the neck. The second policeman lifted his head. His hand came up to his neck, as if to check for an irritating insect bite. He faltered, falling atop his dead colleague.

Speed was now of the essence. His client had paid top dollar for detailed information about this safe house and James expected to find three male protection officers, the mark, and an infant. That meant one more policeman inside. With no gunfire or sounds of a struggle, the remaining officer might not suspect foul play.

James glanced toward the car and saw Maloney staring at the scene with wide eyes. Things had just gotten real for the traitor. James hoped Judas wouldn't take flight while he remained inside completing the contract. He would just have to take that risk. For now, the traitor had work to do to earn his blood money. James pointed meaningfully at the two bodies. The corrupt detective nodded, opening the car door.

James crossed the driveway and entered the foyer, closing the front door behind him. Inside, the air felt pleasantly cool. Walking into the living room, the scent of wild spring flowers welcomed him. *Vogue* magazines lay neatly stacked upon a low, walnut coffee table in front of a large, leather couch.

Unlike hitmen in most movies, James did not draw his gun and move around the building as if he were a hunter stalking deer. Instead he unsheathed his most formidable weapon…his smile. He sauntered around the house as if he were an expected guest.

"Hello," he shouted, "anyone home?"

James entered a dining room furnished with an oak table and six chairs. There was no sign of the third officer. Perhaps the remaining man would come to him if he dallied here.

Stroking the top of a chair, he admired the craftsmanship. It smelled faintly of beeswax. As he traced the petals of a carved rose, a man entered the room. The muscular, black-haired newcomer pointed his Glock straight at James. "Who're you?" he demanded. "Where's Hoffman?"

"I'm Lieutenant Stevenson." James leaned against the chair. "I have a few questions for your witness related to a new case we're working on over in Vice."

The young officer looked him up and down. He seemed puzzled, and didn't lower his weapon.

"Hoffman's just outside." James straightened, but kept his hands away from his own gun. "He's talking with Sergeant Maloney."

Once more James displayed his special simple smile. The officer hesitated, staring at him for a second, and then relented. James saw his smile reflected in the young man's blue eyes before they dipped down as he holstered his Glock.

"Come on. Let's see what's holding up Hoffman," said James as he turned towards the living room, but then paused. He turned to the young man. "You never said your name." James offered his hand.

"Detective Milligan," the officer responded, "Steve Milligan." He grasped James's hand.

A familiar look of shock and panic entered Milligan's eyes. Younger and stronger than the previous two officers, Milligan didn't immediately fall. Instead he opened his mouth to yell. James covered Milligan's mouth with his free hand. Milligan struggled to escape James's grip. He grasped James's right wrist and twisted, digging into James's soft veins and tendons with a hard thumbnail.

However, James had a high pain threshold and a wrestler's grip. He didn't let go as the poison took its delayed effect. Milligan dropped to his knees, and then tumbled onto the bare dining room floorboards. James smiled down at the foolish youth, and released his hand.

James tiptoed into an adjacent room where he discovered toddlers' toys neatly tidied away onto shelves and picture books stacked on a bright yellow bookshelf. At first he detected no signs of life. Then a small, blue door in one corner of the room creaked as it opened a fraction. It looked like it led into a cupboard. James spun and pulled the gun from his holster with his left hand. Most people didn't realize he fought left-handed. It gave him an edge in any fight. He cautiously approached the door and pushed it fully open with his foot.

He stumbled as a black cat sprang out from behind the door and flew between his legs. It hissed and escaped into the dining room. James's heart raced as he cursed the animal. He hated cats because they needlessly tortured their victims. A quick, clean kill was more efficient.

The cupboard was bare. James took deep calming breaths as he continued the room-to-room search. He heard a clattering noise from a further room, so stepped in that direction. Hiding the Glock behind his back, James stepped into a modern, white-tiled kitchen. An aroma of fresh coffee filled the air.

At first, he didn't see what had caused the noise. Then he realized the door of the double-width refrigerator stood open, concealing someone. A hand appeared on its edge, with long, red nails. The door closed, revealing a woman struggling to hold an infant boy and a bag of carrots at the same time.

James instantly recognized his mark: a slim lady in her mid-twenties with long, brunette hair, ample breasts, and a gorgeous face...a stereotypical Godfather's moll.

In the photographs provided by his client, the target had been dressed in designer evening dresses. She looked just as classy today in her flimsy summer dress. Miss Mary Rossi wanted out, but there was only one way out of a relationship with a man like Angelo Carboni.

She glanced at him. "Coffee?"

Mary must have assumed he was another protection officer, one of the countless numbers of defenders who had walked in and out of her life over the past few months. Knowing the job neared completion, he allowed himself to relax. He brought the gun around from behind his back. Peering deep into her eyes, he smiled.

Mary returned his smile with a simple one of her own—a smile warm enough to melt the ice in any executioner's heart. Her face radiated love and compassion. She shifted the boy into her right arm and kissed his forehead.

He raised his weapon. A gentle squeeze of the Glock's sensitive trigger and he would successfully complete another well-paid contract. James hesitated. He found himself focusing on her sweet, cherry-red lips.

A loud gunshot shook the room. Stabbing agony ripped into his stomach. James's eyes widened and he glanced down to Mary's hands. In her left hand she held a smoking gun. Her left hand! A split second later a second shot turned his ribcage into a torture chamber of pain. The Glock slipped from his grasp and landed with a clatter as dense polymer hit stone.

James glanced down. Blood gushed from gaping holes in his chest and stomach. He attempted to stem the flow with his hands. His wounded heart pounded inside a damaged cage. He felt weak and his legs buckled. A third gunshot thundered in his ears. The bullet punched him in the chest and pushed him backward. He plummeted to the floor. His head smashed against something hard. The ceiling dominated his vision.

A blurred Madonna and child drifted into his field of vision and hovered above him. The intense agony raging throughout his chest and gut made any movement torture, yet James stretched toward Mary's legs with his grasping right hand. Never before had he failed to complete a contract. If only he could reach her bare ankles, one touch would complete his task and he could die with an unblemished record.

Mary stepped backward, shaking her head. She smiled and her lips moved. His dying brain struggled to attribute meaning to the sounds they made.

"When you've lived with a dangerous man like Angelo Carboni, you learn never to rely on men for anything …especially protection."

James drifted off into darkness, now beyond pain, a single thought dominating his mind. *Isn't it amazing what a simple smile can achieve?*

The Gun

Megan Arkenberg

Megan is a student in Milwaukee, Wisconsin, where she writes speculative fiction and short-form poetry. Her work has recently appeared in or been accepted for issues of *The Willows*, *MindFlights*, *Beneath Ceaseless Skies*, and *Ideomancer*. She also edits the fantasy e-zine *Mirror Dance* (mirrordancefantasy.blogspot.com).

159

She was smaller than I expected. Propped in her chair like a child's doll, the chains pinning her wrists to the arms seemed to be the only things holding her up. Her stringy, reddish hair gave shape to her face, a white teardrop with two purple bruises for eyes. I did not need to look into those bruises. Every tight, trembling line of her body told me she knew; she was going to die.

I lifted my gun from the table. It had been sitting directly beneath the heat vent throughout the hottest months of the year. Somehow, I'd expected it to retain that warmth.

It felt like ice in my hand.

"What time is it?" Her voice echoed in the low-ceilinged basement, calling to me from all sides. I knew what she was asking.

"We have thirteen minutes left."

She laughed: it was not humourless. The fact that she could find anything funny in the situation made me want to vomit.

"*We?*" Her eyes sparkled coldly. "Who's killing who?"

"Five A.M. on Sunday, April fourth, 2108," I recited. "Zephra Listrata of the Grey Resistance to be hung before delegates of the Global Peace Party for crimes against harmony." I pressed my finger against the trigger. "For crimes against their power."

I laid the gun against her forehead. It left no mark on her skin—not even a shadow. "Five A.M. Sunday, April fourth, 2108. Ismene Eudocia of the GPP to be shot in the basement of the Grey Resistance. No witnesses."

Ismene closed her eyes and opened them, clenched her fists and relaxed them again. "And what is my crime?"

"Not fulfilling your purpose as a hostage," I said. "If the GPP wanted you alive, they should have released Zephra."

She said nothing, only leaned back in her chair. I lowered the gun and went to stand against the table.

"What time is it now?"

I looked at my watch. "Four forty-eight. We have twelve minutes."

"You've never killed before, have you?"

I thought of the bombs, of the raids on GPP spy-houses. Could I be that—a terrorist who'd never killed before? Did such a thing exist?

Her black eyes narrowed. "Don't lie to a dead woman."

I looked at my hand resting on the scarred tabletop. My knuckles were still white from my grip on the gun. "I won't lie to you," I said. "This is my first."

"I'm flattered." Her voice held no mockery, only weariness. "But why you?"

"Why me? Why *me*?" I slammed my fist on the table. "Why *you*? What did you do to get yourself here? That's what you should be asking."

She looked down at the floor, at the white concrete beneath her soft white shoes. *Ismene Eudocia*, I said to myself, to see what the name sounded like in the back of my mind. *Ismene, the woman in the chair in front of me. The woman I'm going to kill.*

I wondered if, in the basement of the Global Peace building, someone was thinking the same thing about Zephra.

"Seven minutes." I reached for the gun again, but stopped myself before I could take it. Why should I? Why should I lengthen my contact with the thing that would...what?

"That's the thing about guns." Ismene had crossed her legs and straightened in the chair, as if preparing for a photograph. "They don't change. What happens to a gun when it kills a man? It empties. Nothing more. It can be loaded again. Guns don't change when they've killed a man—men do."

"Shut up," I said. There was a nauseous feeling in the pit of my stomach, like everything was moving faster than it should be, faster than my eyes could follow. I glanced at my watch. Its

161

face swam before my eyes, and it took me a moment to read. "Five minutes."

She looked down at her lap, as if making sure the fabric of her skirt lay properly. "What's your name?"

"Why does it matter?"

"Why doesn't it?"

"That's a ridiculous answer." I laughed softly, without humour. "My name is Angelos Siphorous."

"Why aren't you picking up the gun, Angelos?"

"We still have five minutes."

Ismene began to rearrange herself, uncrossing her legs, slanting lower in her chair. The chains rattled softly around her wrists. It was the first sign she gave of dis-comfort. "That gun isn't going to make you a murderer, you know."

"Is that really how you want to spend your last five minutes? Convincing me that I'm not a murderer?"

"I never said you weren't. I said the gun wasn't going to make you one."

"Then what is?"

She said nothing, just held my gaze unblinkingly. I looked away first.

"I have a child," she whispered. "Three years old. His name is—"

"I don't care what his name is." I turned to her with a snarl. "Don't you understand that? It doesn't matter if you make me feel sorry for you. I can't change your fate."

"I know." She shrugged, rustling the fabric over her thin shoulders. "It's just...the gun. Funny how you think of things like that."

"Things like what?"

A thin line appeared between her eyebrows. "The GPP has us give them toy guns, you know. They learn early who to hate. My son runs around the house like a mad thing, screaming 'Kill the Greys! Kill the Greys!' It's funny, that I always told him not to."

I glanced again at my watch. "Only a minute left..."

"Don't change the conversation."

"All right." I extended my hands, startled at how the sheen of sweat glistened in the light from the bare bulb. "You want the truth? I'm glad you won't be there to teach your son how to hate us."

"I won't need to teach him, Angelos. You're doing that for me."

Thirty seconds. Did she realize that? I lifted the gun again, took in the feeling of the cold, smooth metal. Twenty seconds. I walked over and pressed it to her temple.

She didn't stop smiling.

Fifteen seconds. Ten seconds. I found myself counting under my breath. Five seconds. The clocks began to chime five o'clock. Three seconds...

"Angelos," Ismene whispered. "What is my crime?"

Two seconds. One.

I pulled the trigger.

"Your crime?" The gun dropped from my numb hand. "You made me a murderer."

The Voices

Karla Cruz

Karla Cruz, an accomplished musician (with a guest appearance with the Seattle Symphony on violin) and singer, has released two of her own CDs. She tackled writing when she found she was dissatisfied with most of what she bought at the bookstores. Writing fiction was a way out of crippling depression and a chance to right life's injustices for Karla. She describes her work as part madcap romp, part transcendence. She loves when a book truly provides exquisite escapism.

In 2007, she published the book *Dog-Almighty!*, a collection of humour essays dealing with chronic depression. *"Think of it as Dave Barry meets William Styron."* The book is available on Amazon.com. She hopes to have the sequel, *Dogs in Trouble!*, completed in 2010. For samples of her current works in progress, visit her website www.karlacruzwriter.com.

He knew I was afraid of heights, which was why he planned my surprise birthday party at the Space Needle. He pushed me in my wheelchair, blindfolded, through the parking lot, to the elevator, and into the hushed restaurant. I felt the panic rising in me as the elevator shot up, but I could do nothing.

He knew I couldn't protest because I was mute. When he took my blindfold off, they were all there, shouting "Surprise!" The confetti flew, and the hired combo struck up "Happy Days Are Here Again".

Everyone was celebrating my birthday and my release from the coma.

He was afraid I was really me inside, even though the doctors said I had amnesia and could not remember my own name. I would not let him know that I knew who I was.

The senator was powerful and had many friends. He had the charisma of Kennedy and the looks of George Clooney, and all the women gushed over him and all the men rushed to be the first to shake his hand. He'd been on CNN, Letterman, and Leno because he was the man to see, to hear, to learn from. More astute than Dr. Phil, shrewd enough to broker deals with foreign corporations that other powerful entities had failed at time and again. They said our country's economy depended on this man—J.J. Carter, my husband.

He had known a major change was coming in my life and had poisoned me before I could get to my lawyers.

I lay in a drug-induced coma for days. My husband told them I had tried to commit suicide.

"Poor Christina. She has bravely battled her depression, her schizophrenia for years. She heard voices all the time. No one fought harder than she did." He shed tears for the cameras as he said these words.

It was true I heard voices. But they always told me the truth. J.J. always said I heard demons. J.J. was what everyone called my boyish husband, he of the perfect white teeth. J.J. didn't believe that the voices I heard were truthful.

So? I looked into the mirror and I heard them. It was me talking back at me, he said. Well, that much was true. There was something inside, fighting for my sanity.

"He means to kill you," the voices said.

I brushed my hair and listened. But I didn't believe them at the time.

"Why should he?" I asked my reflection.

"You know why," the voices said. "Stop playing dumb. The only reason he married you was for your fortune."

"But I have no fortune," I told the girl in the mirror. The girl who looked back at me.

"You don't yet, but believe us, believe us. We know."

"He has enough money," I protested.

"He will never have enough money," they said to me.

The voices were right. I hadn't known, but I was about to receive a huge inheritance on my thirtieth birthday from my Aunt Beatrice. At the time I hadn't even known I had an Aunt Beatrice. But my husband knew. He knew things about me I never dreamed of. And me—so gullible, so naïve. I thought I was crazy because J.J. said it often enough, and I didn't heed the voices.

But the day I received the letter from Beatrice's lawyer was the day J.J. mixed my evening drink for me. And I didn't wake up. Too bad for him I didn't die, but I didn't yet know that was the intention. I thought something had gone horribly wrong with my medication.

I heard him as he talked to me. He thought I couldn't hear, while the respirator breathed for me and the IV fed me.

"In time, Christina, in time," he whispered, as he dared stroke my lifeless hand. "Aunt Beatrice has set me up for life. Oh, yes. And maybe I failed you this time, but I won't next time. I promise," he said as he grinned.

But the voices spoke to me, too. "We will get you out of this. All of us."

"How can there be so many of you inside me? Am I really crazy?" I argued with my voices.

"There are many of us inside you, because there are many of you. Aren't you the poet? Aren't you the violinist? Do you not have a passion for gardening? You give cold, homeless creatures hot chocolate on winter days. You do laundry. You make cookies. You volunteer at the Food Bank. You pray. You sing."

"But—," I argued soundlessly.

"You have been taught not to trust yourself, your own voices. Christina, you must fight for yourself. We are here for you."

And one day I woke from my coma. A miracle, the doctors said. "But she will suffer amnesia and it may be irreversible."

They were wrong. I did not suffer amnesia, but I could not speak and I could not use my legs. I could not use my arms. I could move my fingers a tiny bit, but that was it.

My husband had to feed me, but he quickly grew weary of it and hired a nurse. I was glad. I didn't like him spooning me Jell-O and whispering, "Wonder what I put in this, Christina?"

My thirtieth birthday was now upon me and I knew I was about to become very rich. J.J. had not shown me the letter. But he had mentioned it. He was granted power of attorney over my affairs when I had fallen into the coma.

As I looked blankly at my birthday guests, I heard one of my voices in my head. "Look for the girl with the red hair."

I couldn't turn my head, but as J.J. wheeled me around, I saw her. She was sipping champagne and was quite alone. J.J. wheeled me over to her.

"Simone, this is Christina," he introduced us. "Simone is my right hand."

Simone smiled at me. "J.J., your wife is so beautiful," she said warmly.

"Too bad it's wasted, isn't it?" he quipped.

"That remark is unbecoming of you," Simone chided, frowning.

Simone grasped my still hands gently. "You are very lovely, Christina, and I'm pleased to meet you."

"You realize she can't hear any of this, don't you?" J.J. said.

"You're completely wrong, J.J. Hearing is the last thing to go, and becomes heightened when other senses fail," said Simone.

J.J. must have looked panicked because Simone said, "What's the matter, J.J.? You look like a ghost walked over your grave."

The voices said, "Trust her."

I tried very hard to look at Simone, to send a message with my eyes, but I failed. Her countenance registered no change.

"I work with your husband, Christina. He's quite the mover and shaker. Why, what's wrong? You look like you're about to cry."

She had seen it! She had seen my face! I tried so hard to move my mouth, but nothing but drool slipped past my lips.

~

He knew I was afraid of wild animals and the next weekend he took me to the zoo. He parked my wheelchair right next to the Siberian Tiger cage and he left me. He left me!

A park attendant came by and spoke to me. Of course I couldn't answer. He saw my ID and used his walkie-talkie to radio in a lost visitor.

"Oh, there you are!" J.J. mimicked relief when he showed up. "She just wheels herself off and then I can't find her," he claimed, clearly exasperated, to the park attendant. "She thinks it's a game, but it nearly gives me a heart attack!"

I cried then. A real tear slipped out of my eye. I could actually feel it! Feel it course down my cheek. I didn't want him to see. I didn't want him to think I was coming back. Even if it was in tiny increments. No. I could not let him know!

Simone told me, assuming either I knew or didn't care, that J.J. had bought a beachfront cottage. She fell into the habit of coming by to visit every Monday and she was kind enough to bring me fresh flowers every time.

169

J.J. wasted no time spending my money. Along with the cottage, he bought a boat. He bought not one Jaguar, but two. He bought expensive pieces of jewellery and took delight in showing them to me, explaining that one was for Tiffany, one was for Leticia, another for Simone.

Simone brought back the emerald necklace. She gave it to me one Monday.

"Look, I know you're trapped in there, but you're still beautiful, and you deserve to be ornamented, my dear. Jewels really aren't my thing. You look like you're going to cry again. Oh my God, you are crying!"

She whisked a tissue out and dabbed my cheeks. "I wish you could tell me what is hurting you, Christina."

I wish, too, oh how I wish.

"Do you even know you're Christina? Oh, now I've frightened you. Enough. I'm sorry."

~

My wheelchair was in the library the next time Simone visited me. It wasn't J.J. who'd had the decency to move me, it was the nurse. Simone brought me gardenias.

"I can tell you like these," she said as she placed the luscious-smelling bouquet in front of me.

"You know," she mused. "People can come out of these things all at once or a little at a time. I wouldn't give up hope, Christina. And yes, I know you're in there—I had a dream. A group of ladies came to me in my dream and they said you were still Christina and that I was to help you and, well, I'm a fierce believer in dreams." Here, she wrapped her warm fingers around my cold hands.

"And so I will help you in any way I can."

Don't tell J.J. Don't tell J.J. Please.

"What's the matter? You look concerned. You and I have to figure out a way to communicate. I know you can cry...hmm. Can you move your eyelids? Your eyes?"

I tried.

"You did! You moved them. You crinkled them, like you're mad or something." Simone was excited. "Okay, we've got something here. Crinkle means no. No crinkle means yes. Do you know who you are?" she asked.

No crinkle. Yes.

"Does anyone else know that you know who you are?"

Crinkle. No.

"Not even J.J.?"

Crinkle.

"We should tell J.J."

Crinkle. No!

"No? You don't want him to know?"

Crinkle.

"Jesus, Christina. You seem terrified. I wish you could tell me why."

Me, too. No crinkle.

"You wish you could tell me?"

No crinkle. I tried to move my eyes.

"You moved your eyes! Oh my God, you moved your eyes to the right! Christina, do you know what this means? You're regaining your muscle control. We need to get you to a doctor."

"What's going on in here?" J.J.'s voice boomed.

"She moved her—," but Simone's voice stopped when she saw me crinkle my eyes. "Well, I thought she moved a finger, but I think it was just me twitching," said Simone, recovering brilliantly. She looked at me with true concern, but she knew an exit when she saw it. "I have to get going. Good to see you again, J.J."

~

He knew I was afraid of snakes, so he brought home a huge one in a large cage.

"I've always wanted a snake, but you were always so paranoid of them. You certainly don't need to be afraid anymore, since you don't even know who you are," he chuckled.

He sat the cage on the floor of the library and deliberately left the door to the cage open. "I have a business meeting with Leticia, but I'll be back, Christina. Oh, for certain I'll be back.

Don't worry, you have only a few days left of this madness. You'll stop hearing those voices for sure." And he left.

The huge spotted snake slithered out of its cage. It must have been six feet long. I could feel my breath failing me. I would die of fear, I thought.

The voices came. "You have nothing to fear from this snake. It is not poisonous, it is not dangerous. It is looking for a dark place to hide." The snake slithered under a couch placed under the bay window across the room from me, and I sighed with relief. At least I thought I sighed.

In my fear, I noticed a change in my fingers. They were clutching the arms of my wheelchair. I had moved my fingers!

~

The next Monday Simone came again. This time with Gerbera daisies.

"Okay, let's talk," she began. "It'll be good for you. Do you know how lucky you are to be married to J.J. Carter? That man is hell on wheels." She sighed.

"You're crinkling your eyes—why? Oh my God, your hands! Your hands are clutching the wheelchair! Christina stop! You're going to give yourself cardiac arrest!" Simone's eyes were wide with concern.

"I'd better call an ambulance. I don't want anything to happen to you. You're crinkling your eyes again. No?"

Trust me, I willed her to hear. *Trust me.*

"Okay, let's calm down. Why are you sliding your eyes to the right again? Is there something over there?"

Yes.

"There is! Good girl! Let's play hot and cold. I'll wander about and you tell me yes or no with your eyes. This will be a good game. Good exercise."

It took a dozen times before Simone found the cigar box. She was thrilled when she finally got the "no crinkle" sign from me. She opened it and extracted a two-page folded letter.

"You want me to read this," she stated.

Yes.

172

As Simone's eyes scanned the document, I could see the change on her face. She knew. "Your Aunt Beatrice left you everything . . ." she trailed off as she continued to read. She carefully folded the letter and replaced it in the box. The box J.J. thought I knew nothing about.

"And you can't spend it, can you?" Simone asked.

No.

"What happened, Christina? Did you really try to commit suicide?"

No!

"Oh, Jesus." She held her head in her hands as the full impact hit her.

"What . . . um, what were you given?" she asked.

My eyes slid to the left. She saw the medications. The Valium. The Seconal.

Just then we heard J.J. motor up in his posh, new Jaguar.

"Look. Christina, let me think about this. There's no way I can let on that I know. It's dangerous."

I heard the voices in my head chorusing, "Yes! Yes!"

"Simone," J.J. called to her, as he entered the room. "I've got tickets to a play I thought you might want to see."

"Not in front of Christina, J.J. You know she can hear!" Simone protested.

"Simone, you might as well face facts. For all practical purposes, she's got Alzheimer's," J.J. said without feeling.

"Just the same, J.J., I'd feel a lot better if you took Christina to the play. The stimulation would be good for her. And by the way, do you think she really needs that much sedation? I saw her medication—"

J.J. raised a hand to stop her. "You're not a doctor, Simone. I'm just following orders. But I do appreciate what a good friend you are to her." J.J. turned to look at me, taking in my frail, pathetic, useless form.

"I just hope she doesn't slip back into that coma."

The voices came suddenly. "He's setting you up. He's going to do it again and he's setting the stage."

I knew I didn't have much time. If he could just wait one more week, I just needed to see Simone one more time.

And then my miracle happened. The very next day I could really move my hands. I mean really. I could make a fist. I could move my lower arms. I could move the switches on my wheelchair. The voices urged me on. "Do it, Christina. Do it, if it's the last thing you do!"

One dose at a time. J.J. didn't notice the amount of pills missing from my vials. He assumed the nurse gave them to me as he'd instructed, but as she popped them in my mouth, I was able to slide them under my tongue and when she turned her back, I let them fall out of my mouth onto my lap. When she left the room, I ground each one with a spoon at a low desk in the library, scraped together the tiny granules of each, and dropped them in my robe pocket.

The next Monday, Simone visited me again, bringing me yellow roses.

No.

"What are you saying 'no' for?" she asked. "Oh, you think yellow roses are for a funeral don't you?"

Yes.

"Christina, I need to be frank with you." Simone drew a chair close and whispered. "I am afraid for you, but I don't know what to do and I don't want to cause any trouble."

Just do what I ask you to do.

I slid my eyes to the right.

"The cigar box?"

No.

Simone looked in the direction of the cigar box, her eyes finally resting on the bar in the library.

"The bar? You want a drink?"

Yes.

"What do you want to drink—water, juice?"

No. My arms gripped the armrests and I moved the wheelchair.

"You can move your wheelchair! You really are coming around!"

Simone was overjoyed, but then she noticed the pleading look I tried so hard to convey.

"You want me to help you."

Yes.

"What do you want me to do?"

"Bring her the glass, Simone. Bring her the glass," the voices chanted.

Simone brought an empty glass to me. She set it on my tray. I took the powder out of my pocket, fumbling clumsily. But I got quite a handful and sprinkled it into the glass.

"Wait, Christina, I will not let you try to take your life!" Simone took the glass from me.

No!

"No," she said with certainty. Then her eyes widened. She knew. She carried the glass to the bar.

"Which is it? Tell me."

With my eyes, I told her.

J.J. had a nightly habit of vodka and grapefruit juice, and I knew where he kept it and I knew which glass he used. Simone poured the vodka and the juice.

"I'm home!" J.J.'s voice boomed. He bounced into the library and looked at Simone. "Simone, you are such a gem to keep my lovely wife company. And you poured me a drink! What a sweetheart." He bent to kiss her cheek.

"I've got to go," she stammered, looking at her watch. "I'm already late for a date."

"I hope you're not replacing me," J.J. had the nerve to say in front of me.

"I wish you wouldn't talk like that, J.J." Simone threw her sweater over her shoulders and left.

J.J. studied me intently, his drink in his hands. He looked into his glass. "Murky-looking this time." He turned to the sink to throw it out.

"No!" the voices shrieked. *No,* I mouthed.

"You didn't just say something, did you?" J.J. looked at me curiously. "No, you couldn't, you're so pathetic. This drink needs ice cubes." He turned to the tiny fridge kept under the bar.

I would have glared at him if I could. I would have rushed him with my wheelchair, but I didn't want him to know that I could move; that I could save my life.

175

"Well, I've got a gift for you tonight, Christina. Tonight, I put you out of your misery. For once and for all. But first, I need my little evening pick-me-up."

The Only Way Out

E.H. Rydberg

E.H. Rydberg currently lives in Harrogate, UK, with his Italian wife, British daughter, and Israeli cat, where he enjoys writing speculative fiction and creating digital artwork. His recent publications include stories in *Wanderings* and *Long Story Short* and the 3D digital image *Attack!* in the first issue of *Crossed Genres*. He resides online at www.edwinhrydberg.com where examples of his work can be found.

I could never hurt her.

That thought tortures me again as I stare at a new spider web spanning the pale blue corner of the living room. It's the female spider that is dominant, spinning the webs, using and often devouring the insignificant male. Sometimes she allows him to live in her web for a while, as long as it suits her needs. I've been in this web too long and it feels like she's sucking my life out.

"…right honey?"

The question catches me unaware so I nod, unsure where the conversation has gotten to. Uncaring. She's the one who's good at small talk. I'm just the insignificant male on the web. After the moment's pause the four of them begin chattering again. The mindless drone of words is almost tangible in the warm, stagnant air. I'm suffocating on sound. I need space.

"Anyone want a coffee?" They pause in their verbal vomiting and I register three, including her, and one juice, before I stand, turning toward the kitchen.

"Take this, honey."

A plate of crumbs. I reach for it reluctantly. It's a small thing, but give an inch and she takes a mile. It always seems this way. I take the plate, nod to her guests, and enter the kitchen. As the door swings closed behind me, I take a deep breath, relief almost palpable. Only now, alone, does the pressure ease from my chest.

I could never hurt her. I used to believe that, but I have to do something. Just being in her presence is like running sandpaper over my brain. Her every word, every motion, each tiny nuance drives me insane. It's either her or me.

Before, when I was younger, more naive, I never would have believed myself capable of such thoughts. When you're a kid you wonder what kind of person murders; what type of sick, twisted mind can snuff the life of another. As you grow older you realize it's more about circumstance than predisposition. One day you wake up to find your life has gone down the wrong path. Worse still, you can no longer see the way back. You're not even sure where the right path is. That's when you learn what you're really capable of. That's when you escape the childhood notion "I could never do that" and you come face to face with your own beast within.

Setting the dirty plate on the table I start up the coffee maker. It's one of those deluxe models; cost a fortune. Rule number one in this household—*thou shall never be without coffee*. I don't drink the stuff myself but I learned to run the machine for her.

As the coffee maker is warming up I pull a bowl from the cupboard, placing it onto the countertop. Then I reach to the back of the top shelf above the stove and take down an airtight jar filled with dried leaves. A few tugs and the lid pops loose. There's a curious lack of odour as I shake the leaves from the jar into the bowl. They fall like cornflakes, only not as solid.

Out of habit, one ear focuses on the living room conversation, just audible through the closed door. By nature I'm a little paranoid, but I have no real fear of being caught. Once she starts talking she's like a runaway train; nothing short of a violent collision will stop her.

Next I take out the rolling pin and use the grip as a pestle to grind the leaves. Any crackling is easily drowned by the coffee maker, which is just finishing the first cup. I continue grinding until the leaves are a fine powder.

One tablespoon of water, a teaspoon of vinegar: glacial, white vinegar, not those European malt or wine extracts—don't want any contaminants. Not too much liquid—the concentration has to stay high. I stir the powdered leaves rapidly in the mixture until the crystal clarity becomes a murky green. Finally, mix in a quarter teaspoon baking soda to neutralize the vinegar so the concoction doesn't taste weird.

179

Funny, all those classes in chemistry are useful at last. I laugh to myself. It's almost like being on a cooking show, except there aren't any cameras.

I suppose it's not unusual that now, at the end, my mind drifts back over our history together. I remember my surprise the first time I thought of killing her, the moment I learned I was capable of such thoughts. I had...have...a great respect for all life, from the tiniest insect to the most inane person—a firm belief that all life has a right to exist. Yet there I was thinking thoughts of cold-blooded murder, of intentionally extinguishing the spark of another creature. It was like peering into the twisted mind of a person on the evening news. I didn't like it.

But the thought kept calling to me. It grew stronger day by day, frighteningly so. And it came with a seductive sense of power. For the first time, dangling before me was the promise of escape, a means to leave the trap, the constant misery. It was a new road I could take that wouldn't require admitting my failure. I was afraid, yet eager, to follow.

The mixture is now a runny, green paste. Finally, it's finished. Quality, home brewed. You can't just buy this stuff from your local grocer. The spoon stutters against the bowl and I steady my shaking hand.

Breathe. Stay calm. A few drops in the coffee and it will all be over. One...two...three for good measure. Enough to do the deed; not enough to be traced. Each drop falls like a slowing heartbeat until it collides with the brown mirrored surface, sending transient colours rippling across the coffee before the cup is still once again.

How like life is a cup of coffee—dark and bitter unless you add enough milk and sugar.

Unfortunately, unlike coffee you don't always know what's missing in your life. You try to analyze it and, logically, everything seems fine. One plus one equals two, equals happily ever after. Except it doesn't. And you don't know why.

I pour the remaining mixture down the drain, rinsing it away with hot water before washing the spoon and bowl. No paper trail. Perhaps that's my fatal flaw—an over-developed desire to be mysterious, to be different, to stand out from the drab sameness I see in commuter eyes every day.

I will miss her, even now. Even when every moment is torturous there is still something, some accident of nature that calls me to her. Strange, I've always had more pleasant thoughts of her when we were apart. Somehow the memory of her smile is stronger than the real thing.

I shake my head, force myself to stay in the moment. Best do it now, before my nerve is lost.

"Honey, everything okay?" she calls from the living room. That she's noticed my absence is a sure sign I've been taking too long.

Now, at the end, I find the good memories. Laughs shared during romantic dinners, staring deep into love-filled eyes on quiet walks, passionate mornings lasting until noon. How have those beautiful moments led to this? Is there anything of them remaining? Maybe. But I've made my decision and it's too late to back out because of unlikely possibilities.

"Just fine," I answer. My voice is steady but the cup is shaking in my hand as I lift it.

Raising the steaming liquid to my lips, I choke back a large swig. And another. The vile stuff is more bitter than I thought. But the coffee is the least of my concerns. The poison acts fast. Numbness deadens my arm and I drop the cup. In the haze of my fading vision I watch as it smashes on the linoleum floor.

"Honey? Are you okay?" There is a worried edge to her voice this time.

I try to call out, leave her with some false reassurance, but my voice fails as I crumple to the floor.

It was never her. I realized that eventually. It was me. I was the one who couldn't cope. I was the one with the problem. How could I snuff the beautiful spark of life from another person to pay for my weakness?

I will miss her. She was always my better half. I could never hurt her.

XDA Za: The Wild Hunt

Jason Franks

Jason Franks writes fiction and code. His prose fiction work has been published in *Deathlings* and *Badass Faeries 2: Just Plain Bad*. His comics work, illustrated by artists from Australia, the USA, France, and Japan, has appeared in *Robots are People*, *Inkslinger*, *Tango*, and a number of others. He runs the small press comics imprint Blackglass Press. Franks currently lives in Melbourne, Australia. Visit him online at www.jasonfranks.com.

I'm utterly exhausted when I get off the plane in Mesra City. Starting in Tokyo and connecting in London, Paris, and Boston, it's easily a fifty-hour commute from my front door to the office on that ridiculous itinerary. But this is Mesra City, and the only way to get here is the long way. I should be used to it by now.

When I come out of passport control there's a man holding a sign with my name written on it in kanji. It's not the script that surprises me, it's the fact that there is somebody here at all. It's unusual and imprudent for anybody connected with my firm to meet me in public.

The man has the dark skin and pale eyes of a local, but he's dressed in a suit that seems archaic for this unusual part of the world. When I approach him he bows to me uncertainly. I return the bow and wave off his offer to haul my luggage.

"Do you speak Japanese?" I venture. "English?" I'm as surprised to hear one as the other in this place.

"English. I am called Jeeves."

I can't think of anything else to ask, so I say, "Let's go, then."

I sigh when Jeeves takes me to his VTOL limousine cab. I've avoided riding in one of these until now; I always take the train. Lunatic taxi drivers are a given any place you travel to, and the thought of riding with one in this city's crazily-looped, multi-strata expressways makes me sick to my stomach. I get inside and close my eyes.

I'm expecting to get out at the Epsidor, my usual hotel, but instead Jeeves takes me to a shabby-looking restau-rant. This is a part of Mesra City I've never been to before: dingy grey plastic walls, discoloured tiles, exposed plumbing, bizarre-looking satellite dishes, and antennae on the rooftops.

"Mister is inside waiting for you," says Jeeves. "You can leave your luggage with me."

No question who Mister is; there's only one person here who could have sent an English-speaking cab driver named Jeeves to collect me. I wonder if Miz will be there as well. The cab remains parked out front of the restaurant as I go inside—looks like this is going to be a short meeting.

The maitre d' is wearing shorts and a tank top. He approaches and says something to me in Karachidaean. In English I reply, "Um, Mister Smith?"

I made the name up, but it has the desired effect. "English," he says, and guides me to a table at the back of the room.

My boss has that smug, well-fed, over-tanned look of a Londoner on holiday in some warmer clime where the currency favours the pound sterling. This is exactly what he is, except he's not on holiday—he's just an asshole. He's by himself, tonight; no sign of his Karachidaean business partner 'Miz'.

"Have a seat, Mister Zai," he says to me, gesturing and smiling broadly. He doesn't offer to shake my hand. I bow and take the offered seat.

"I'm afraid I'll have to keep this brief, we're running on a very short time frame this time." The Englishman pauses and looks over my shoulder. "Ah, there we are."

A waiter is approaching with a small steel bowl containing what appears to be a serving of Italian ice cream…if gelato were made with dry ice. When the waiter sets the bowl down I fight the urge to snap a photograph of it on my camera phone.

The waiter looks at me, but the Englishman waves him off. "This gentleman won't be staying to eat."

That's more than fine. I just want to get to the hotel and have a shower; I'm certainly not going to miss the Englishman's company. The Englishman tucks into his dessert with a spoon. Around a mouthful of hot ice cream he says to me, "So tell me, Mister Zai, do you feel up to killing a god?"

I don't reply immediately, but he can tell that I'm not keen on the idea. It's not the god part that concerns me; it's the visibility of the hit. Killing a god is one thing; getting away with it is quite another.

The Englishman flips me a photograph of a line drawing. "The client." A one-eyed man with a thick beard, wearing a wide-brimmed hat. "You recognize him?"

"No."

"His name is Odin, or Wotan or Woden, like that. He used to be the All-Father of Norse myth, but he fucked that up, didn't he? He's a world-class arsehole, this one."

I nod. I'm completely uninterested in an appraisal of my client's character.

"The other gods in his pantheon—the Aesir— demoted him to a sort of folk hero. This led to a few episodes of self-mutilation and eventually a suicide attempt...I guess the geezer just wanted some attention. It worked, unfortunately. He's made a bit of a come-back...but even that was short lived. Bit of a novelty hit, in other words."

"But he's still a god?"

"Yes, indeed. And he does have a small handful of arsehole worshippers. That's why the customer wants him removed."

"Where can I find him?"

The Englishman flips a plastic envelope stuffed with tickets across the table to me. "These tickets will get you right up close," says the Englishman. "A genuine Wild Hunt, led by Odin himself."

"A Wild Hunt?"

"He really is down on his luck," says the Englishman, grinning. "But the tickets are pretty exclusive. Odin will lead a band of wealthy Karachidaean tourists on a pillage-and-plunder raid through the skies of scenic Northern Europe, followed by drinks and a meal against the aurora borealis backdrop."

It's starting to sound a bit more plausible. The hit will take place in a particularly remote part of the usual world. Any witnesses will be violent, thrill-seeking tourists from a country that doesn't exist. Best of all, the client is himself a myth.

I take the envelope and inspect the contents. A fistful of airline tickets and printouts and a small stone covered with runic script.

"The hunt departs from the Dimmuborgir in Iceland, nine pm on the fifteenth, local time."

I blink a couple of times. "Three days."

The Englishman grins. "On your bike, then, sunshine. Jeeves is waiting to take you back to the airport."

The itinerary back to the usual world is worse than the one that brought me here. Of course, I have to take the long way back—I think it's some kind of condition for visiting the unusual part of the world where Mesra City is located.

Mesra City to Buenos Aires isn't so bad, but by the time I hit Austin I'm starving. Worse, I've got severe diarrhoea from eating nothing but airline food for days. During my three-hour layover I find a Tex-Mex restaurant in the airport. I already have diarrhoea, so what does it matter? I order big. It's processed chain restaurant fare, but so delicious to me that I take half a dozen photos of the meal in various states of disrepair and I buy a bottle of hot sauce on the way out.

I connect to San Francisco, then Vladivostok and Helsinki. By the time I make it to Reykjavik I am delirious from sleep deprivation, dehydration, and minor food poisoning.

I would, under most circumstances, be excited to be visiting a new country. I've just come back from Mesra, the city that arose when Atlantis fell. I've ridden the Space Whip into orbit. I sojourned in Faerieland. I've stayed in a medieval resort village and a dirigible city. Am I jaded now? Am I so spoiled that Iceland seems uninteresting?

No, I decide, I'm just really, really sick.

I collect my baggage and find a bench on which to collapse. After ten minutes of staring into space I open the folder of tickets that the Englishman gave me to see what's next. One good thing about being back in the usual world—everything is in English, not Karachidaean. Japanese would be better, but in this state I would struggle even with my native tongue. It takes me half an hour to work out how I'm supposed to get to the rendezvous for the hunt.

187

The Englishman has arranged a rental car for me. I'm supposed to drive to the other side of the country and check into a small resort hotel—the rendezvous point for an 11 pm start the following evening—where he has generously left me about six hours to sleep off the flight.

Not likely.

I throw away the car voucher and check into the airport hotel. In my room I pop five Lomotil tablets and three Ibuprofen, take a long, hot shower, and collapse in bed for fifteen hours.

The following morning I still can't face breakfast. I buy myself a bulky anorak in the hotel gift shop. The anorak has fur at the sleeves and on the hood, and prints of cute walruses all over it. Ready to face the elements, I go off to ask the concierge about chartering a helicopter.

I get paid pretty well for the work I do, so I've never asked for expenses before…but that's about to change. It's not that I can't afford to hire the chopper; it's the Englishman's attitude. It's the smile on his face when he handed me that envelope and sent me back to the airport.

I'm not a violent person. I don't enjoy seeing others suffer, although I admit that I'm not particularly offended by it, either. I don't believe in justice or karma or much of anything, really. I've never felt the need to revenge any slights or indignities, deliberate or accidental. But if, somehow, the Englishman were to become one of my clients…

I don't kill people that I know for a number of very good reasons, but I think, if the need were to arise, I would make an exception for the Englishman.

While I wait for my chopper I surf the web on my phone. I skim the first paragraphs of the Wikipedia entry for Odin but it's not very interesting or relevant. The client is the client; it doesn't matter who they are or what they did as long as they wind up dead. I spend most of my time reading about Iceland; the geography, the sights, the people, the cuisine. I wish I had a Lonely Planet book, but I don't really have time for that anyway. I'll pick one up after the job and spend a few days travelling around.

The chopper is ready sooner than I had expected, so I take the pilot up on his offer to show me some highlights on the way to the rendezvous site. There's a lot to take in: glaciers and fjords, volcanoes, waterfalls, barren arctic deserts. Green and grey and black, a lot less snowy whiteness than I had expected. There isn't a lot of light remaining—the days are terribly short here in winter— but it takes a long time for what light there is to vanish altogether. I fill up a memory card taking photos through the cabin windows.

Eventually the chopper sets down at the rendezvous site, the Dimmuborgir, which the pilot tells me means "Dark Fort". It's a massive and jagged formation of volcanic rock that's lit up by some concealed spotlights in the best tourist-attraction tradition. It stinks of sulphur, and the chopper pilot tells me that clouds of gas issue from the chimneys sometimes. Trolls and monsters live in the caves below it, he says; it's supposed to be a gateway down to hell. "But you already knew that, didn't you?"

"I just thought it was a tourist site."

"You're not a…music fan…?"

"I like music," I reply, confused.

The pilot shakes his head and pops the doors. I take a dozen or so photos before I join the other tourists.

The eleven tourists are waiting on the scree, huddled by what looks like a temporary shelter. A noisy diesel generator provides electricity for a large outdoor heater. Most of the others are Karachidaean, but not all of them. A pair of Swedes—one fat, one skinny—and a Polish skinhead in a greatcoat round out the group.

My arrival by helicopter does not impress anybody. None of the other tourists greet me when I stamp from the cold and sidle up to the heater, but a cheerful man wearing a name badge emerges from behind the shelter and waddles up to me. When I show him the rune stone from the Englishman's packet he claps his hands and says "Oh good, we're all here!" He repeats this in German and then, I think, in Danish. "Welcome, Oskorei, to the Dimmuborgir!"

A smattering of glove-muffled applause.

"The Wanderer will be here soon with your mounts and weapons and the hunt will commence," the host continues.

"You will fly with him around the south coast, across the Norwegian and Northern Seas, and then over Deutschland, Danmark, and Polska. You will pass over the Baltic Sea, along the west coast of Finland, and then across the northern parts of Sverige, and finally to Norge. The Father of Victory will conduct periodic stops at various locations where you will be encouraged to wreak whatever mayhem you desire with your special weapons.

"During your flight you will experience time dilation effects similar to those which Father Christmas is said to undergo. This will be a fabulous and exhilarating experience that I am sure you will be telling your friends and family about for many years to come.

"The Hunt will end in Norway with a bonfire and a meal by the Northern Lights, and an opportunity to socialize in an informal setting. We will be serving traditional food...reindeer stew...and if you managed to bring any game our chefs will help you to cook that as well. There will also be a vegetarian option.

"The All-Father will then depart and a hup swhaber collect you and your trophies safely back to Reykjavik."

The group have a lot of questions about the animals and the weapons and the "hup swhaber". I keep my grumpiness to myself. I'm still tired and a bit run down and now I have to go on a guided tour at night in the freezing cold with a group of obnoxious tourists.

Suddenly, the group falls silent. A spotlight swivels and I turn around to see what everyone is looking at: a lone figure walking up the road, leaning on a spear. A tall man wearing a long coat and a broad-brimmed hat. The figure comes up the scree towards us, slow but sure-footed.

Despite the hokey entrance, Odin cuts an impressive figure; grim and self-assured, he's seven feet tall, with long, grey-blonde hair. His face is a livid red mess around his missing eye, but the remaining orb gleams bright and sharp, and seems unusually mobile in its socket. I'm surprised at the stubbly chin; the drawing I was shown indicated a beard. He reeks of blood and leather.

This is the first time I've ever felt physically intimidated by a client.

Odin does not greet us. He turns his head towards the massive black rock formation and raises his spear, then slams the butt onto the ground.

Sulphurous steam billows from the rocks and I cover my nose and mouth with my hands. Thunder rumbles ominously, followed by a high-pitched shrieking. Twelve beasts gallop down out of the sky: mostly horses, but there are a couple of boars and goats amongst them. Their hooves strike sparks from the rocky ground, even though they're unshod. The animals snort and snuffle into a semicircle behind Odin, breath steaming, tongues of flame and coils of lightning playing across them.

Odin indicates that we form up. When we have shuffled into something resembling a single rank the Wanderer opens his coat and produces a short, heavy sword made of soft iron. He gives this to the first person in the line, who bows timidly and takes it.

Odin makes his way down the line, handing out swords and spears and axes. One hunter gets a bow and a quiver of arrows. The Polish skinhead accepts a heavy mace, but he shows Odin that he's brought along his own weapon: an AK-47. Odin acknowledges it with approval.

I'm second from the end of the line. When it's my turn, I smile up at the All-Father as if I don't quite understand what's going on. I'm the shortest man in the group and he gives me a look of derision when he produces a long knife from inside his coat. I shake my head and open my anorak.

"Kamera!" I point to the instrument hanging around my neck and nod vigorously. "I will take photo!"

Odin curls his lip and grunts dismissively. He gives the knife to the last man in the line. When we are all appropriately armed Odin directs each person in the line to a particular mount.

The mount I've been assigned is the smallest and tamest of the beasts. When the host comes to help me onto it I ask him, "What kind of goat is this?"

The host shakes his head, grinning. "This is not a goat," he says. "It's an Icelandic sheep."

It takes a bit of an effort to get onto my hunting sheep. The animal is compliant enough, but the saddle is a bit unusual. Once my feet are in the stirrups the host helps to secure me with an array of additional nylon straps, buckles, karabiners, and Velcro tabs.

I'm the last one ready. The animals paw at the ground restlessly while Odin discards his hat and shrugs off his coat. He's bare-chested beneath it: lean and hairless and covered in scar tissue. A thick burn goes all the way around the bicep of his left arm, and there are bruises all around his neck.

"Sleipnir!" he commands. His voice is high-pitched and musical, but there's a definite tone of menace to it.

A massive grey animal arises behind him, as though from an invisible crevasse in the earth. It looks a bit like an eight-legged horse, at first glance, but the longer I look at it the more it seems to resemble some kind of hideous octopus. Shadows leak from its eyes and its mouth-beak is filled with triangular teeth.

Odin gives me a disapproving, one-eyed stare when I start snapping photos, but he doesn't tell me to stop. He climbs onto Sleipnir's back and waves the spear overhead. Perhaps I'm imagining it, but the octo-horse does not seem to appreciate this very well.

"Oskorei!" he shouts. "We fly! Let the Wild Hunt begin!"

I take some more photos, but I have to stow the camera and grab onto the reins with both hands as my battle sheep canters into the air behind the other hunters.

The Wild Hunt is actually pretty tame compared to the taxi-ride through Mesra City. There's no wind despite the ridiculous speeds at which we are moving. There's no shortage of oxygen. It's not even particularly cold—in fact I'm a lot warmer up here in my anorak than I was on the ground. I can hear the other hunters chatting amongst themselves in their little cliques.

As we skirt along the coast of Iceland and head out over the sea I find that I can observe the ground with perfect clarity. The waves on the water seem to be still. We pass over some fishing trawlers that do not appear to be moving, despite the thick plumes of wake they leave behind them.

Our first stop-off is an oil rig. Odin leads us towards it in a curving descent, shrieking a high-pitched song in some old Norse tongue. Gouts of fire crackle around Sleipnir as he leads us down out of whatever strange magical bubble has kept us alive and healthy and virtually outside of time. I can feel the heat of re-entry, but it seems that the god and his steed have absorbed most of it for us. Now there's wind and cold and motion. My animal's hooves clock against the sky as if it were solid ground; I feel an impact with every footfall.

The hunters scream and laugh and hack and stab at the pylons and cables of the structure as we roar past it. We wheel about and come back for another pass. I don't have to do very much—my mount follows the party without my guidance.

A couple of beardy riggers stumble out onto the deck area, confused and sleepy. The Polish man tries to bring his AK-47 around, but he gets the butt caught in the reins and it tumbles out of his grip. The weapon vanishes into the sea with barely a splash. I'm glad that I no longer have to worry about friendly fire.

One of the Karachidaeans hacks at a rigger with an axe, taking off most of the poor bastard's arm. When we come around for a third pass Odin skewers the remaining rigger with his spear. With one hand he slings the corpse across Sleipnir's saddle and frees the spear. I can't get a good photograph of it; despite my jockeying, the two Swedes keep getting in my way.

We ride on into the night, screaming with joy and fury. I wonder how much longer this is going to go on.

We storm a small Bavarian village. We destroy a large portion of the Øresundsbroen bridge-tunnel which connects southern Sweden to northern Denmark by road and rail. We demolish a hamlet in Poland; we raze a ski resort in Finland. We obliterate a Sami village in the Lappish part of Sweden before we finally cross over the border into Norway. Most of

193

the others have managed to make some kind of kill, and many of them have trophies, but Odin is the only one who's managed to haul a complete carcass back with him. I haven't killed any-one…yet…but I've filled up my remaining memory card with photos.

The terminus of the wild ride is a remote fjord on the Norwegian coast, facing out onto the Barents Sea. The bonfire is already going when we get there, and the "hup swhaber"—a nicely maintained Sikorsky Skyhook—is standing off to one side.

Sleipnir hits the ground first, and Odin is on his own two feet well before the rest of us alight. There are picnic tables, benches, a latrine block, and a sort of a gazebo where a chef has set up a small kitchen. The host who greeted us in Iceland—or perhaps his twin brother—is waiting for us by an enormous bonfire. The chopper's pilots are leaning against their vehicle, smoking. The aurora borealis shimmers in the distance like disco lights behind a wet shower curtain.

I'm the last one on the ground again. The host helps clip me out of my saddle and I climb down off my hunting sheep.

The other hunters are still giddy with excitement. They rush around laughing and shouting, high-fiving and chest-bumping each other, waving their weapons and recalling the highlights of the hunt. The Swedes glance at me a few times, sniggering, but nobody else pays me any attention. When the host announces that the bar is open and the mead is hot, there's a stampede.

I look at the Northern Lights, but not for very long. I've seen them before, and frankly the view was better in Canada.

Odin is also hanging back from the others. I give him a thumbs-up and fumble out my camera, even though the memory card is full. He sneers at me and turns his back. Odin stalks off to retrieve the corpse of the oil rigger from where he has it secured across Sleipnir's back. The octo-horse growls something discourteous at him and he growls back.

Dinner is ready and I join the back of the line of drunken hunters. I'm starving; I haven't eaten anything substantial since Austin. My stomach feels okay for the first time in days.

"More, please," I ask the chef when he spoons a pile of chunky reindeer stew and roasted potatoes on my plate.

Odin is going around, now, asking everybody how they enjoyed the hunt and thanking them for their comradeship. The words are scripted and it's clear that they're bitter on his tongue. We're not proper Oskorei, we're a bunch of tourists and he resents riding with us. I wonder why he agreed to it in the first place. Will none of the real monsters hunt with him anymore? Does he just need the money?

Odin is getting more and more terse as he moves amongst the crowd, meeting his obligations to the tourist company under the host's watchful gaze. The Wanderer's single eye glitters with anger; he's having real trouble keeping his temper in check. I still have no idea how I'm going to kill him.

But first, I need to eat. I find an isolated spot by the fire and sit down to it. I'm so hungry that I shovel down three mouthfuls and almost swallow my spork before I notice how bland it tastes.

I eat a couple more mouthfuls while looking around to see if anybody has a salt cellar or a pepper pot. That's when I remember the hot sauce.

I open the little bottle and stir some of its contents into the stew—carefully. This sauce is marked Extra Hot, and I bought it in Texas. I taste it, add some more, and stir it again. I'm just about to put another sporkful in my mouth when I realize that I have company.

Odin is standing over me, arms folded, and seething with rage. "What are you doing?" he demands in comically musical English.

"Making fu-rai-va?" I give him the big smile that goes with my pidgin English.

"There is not enough *flavour* for you?"

I look away in contemplation, then look back at him. "Eeeh...so-so," I reply, prevaricating in the best Japanese manner.

"This food has nourished generations of hunters!" Odin snarls. "Warriors and rapists and killers and *gods*. But it does not have enough flavour for *you*?"

195

"Not-to ena-fu," I agree, nodding and then shaking my head.

Odin thrusts his face into mine and jabs at me with one long, bony finger. "You insult my hospitality? In my own lodge? After I have shared a hunt with you?" Flecks of his spittle scald my face.

I blink at him. "This is most delicious sauce," I say, holding up the little bottle. It has a picture of a cowboy on it. "Do you wanna try some?"

Odin's mouth works, but he can't find anything to say. His shoulders bunch; I can see that he wants to hit me. I reach up and throw some hot sauce into his single staring eye.

Odin lurches away, screaming. He thrashes around, clawing helplessly at his face. Drunken tourists scatter.

The former All-Father backs into the bonfire, but he doesn't seem to notice—his skin doesn't burn. At least, fire won't burn it. Chilli oil, on the other hand, seems to be quite effective.

Odin staggers around in a circle, wracked with spasms of agony. He starts bellowing for water in half a dozen different Germanic languages, but nobody has the courage to approach him. I'm never going to get a better chance than this, and I'm just trying to work out what to do when his own spear hits him in the face. By the time he falls over, half the length of it is protruding through the back of his skull.

Sleipnir approaches his master's corpse on two legs, six tentacle arms waving from his shoulders. Now he looks a bit more like a bear than an octopus or a horse. He bends down and grabs the butt of the spear, puts one foot on Odin's chest, and hauls the weapon loose. There's not much of a skull left by the time it comes free.

"For fifteen centuries you rode me like I was a horse," says Sleipnir, addressing the corpse, "but who's laughing now, arsehole?" He spits. "*Gungnir* is mine, and so, too, is your life."

He stands there for a full minute before anybody reacts.

"Sleipnir, Sleipnir!" demands one of the Swedes. "Sleipnir, is he truly—"

"'Sleipnir' is not my name," says the eight-limbed monstrosity, turning to face us. "My name is Ehwaz."

Ehwaz tucks the spear under one of his many arms and rises into the sky. "When you repeat this tale, make sure you name me true." His grey skin darkens to black—or perhaps it becomes translucent to the night sky—and the restored god vanishes into darkness.

The hunting party are quite subdued while the host and his crew collect all of the weapons and break everything down. I ask the chef for another plate of stew and a new spork before he throws the leftovers out; it's actually pretty good—with the addition of the hot sauce.

I'm whistling when we find our seats in the chopper for the flight back to Reykjavik. The job is done and my belly is full. There's no urgent requirement for me to get home to Tokyo; it's not like I have a day job to go back to. I ask if anybody has a Lonely Planet guide to Iceland, but nobody answers me. By the time I fall into a doze I'm wondering if I can still use the Englishman's rental car reservation without a copy of the voucher.

Thank you for reading.

If you've enjoyed this anthology, please leave
a review at your favourite retailer.

www.ingramcontent.com/pod-product-compliance
Lightning Source LLC
Chambersburg PA
CBHW020630180626
46816CB00003B/886